THE DAMNED

By

Paul J. Kearns

ISBN:9781739784485

For Carrie, Quinn, and Erin.

This book is a work of fiction. All names, characters, locations, and incidents are either a product of the Author's imagination or are used fictitiously. Any resemblance to actual events, locations, or persons, living, dead or undead, or immortal is purely coincidental.

Any mentions of members of the armed forces in this book are done so with the utmost respect to the people who have and still do serve in the military. Thank you for your service.

Content Warning:
Death, severe injury detail, graphic gore, torture, emotional abuse, drug use, .

Contents

Acknowledgements:
Thank you to Carrie, Quinn, and Erin for all your love and support.
Thank you to my Mum, Dad for bringing me up right, for teaching me that I can shape my own future, and teaching me to go and get what I want from life.
Thank you to Noel and Sam for the ongoing support and for believing in me.
Thank you to Louise Croft for all your help.
Thank you to all my extended family for being there when we have needed you most and for being amazing.
Thank you to all my friends, you know who you are and know I love you.
To Mr. Roberts, my former English teacher at Little lever secondary school as it was back then, thank you for being a great teacher and encouraging me to continue writing fiction.

Also, to you the reader, thank you for reading this book. I appreciate you with all my heart.

Email Paul:
PJKauthor@hotmail.com

Other books by Paul J Kearns:
The Hunted and other Twisted Tales.

Special Operations vampire Elimination Unit

Beasts of Immortality Book 1: Blood and Purpose

Beasts of Immortality Book 2: Armed To The Teeth

You can find Paul J Kearns on social media.
Facebook:
https://m.facebook.com/PJKearnsAuthor/
Instagram:
https://www.instagram.com/pauljkearnsauthor/
Twitter:
www.twitter.com/pjkearnsauthor
and TicTok as PaulJKearns

Aftermath.

I sat in the chair and looked out of the bedroom window of my mum's house. It's something I had found myself doing a lot since I had to move back into my childhood home. Although this room had been mine for many years as a child I didn't feel like I could call it mine anymore. I had moved out fifteen years ago and even though my relationship with my parents was good I just never thought I would have a reason to move back here.

My mum wasn't too happy about it either. Since my dad died she had become fiercely independent.

"I'm doing just fine as I am, thank you," are the words she would say to anyone who tried to offer her help, my sister and myself included.

She hasn't told me so in as many words but I could tell by how little she would talk to me. What little she did say to me would just be spoken out into the air. It was as if she didn't care if I heard her or not. It was strange because she had always been so loving and attentive before I moved back in. I suppose her grief for my dad had changed her.

It's not my fault I had to move back. I loved living in my own home and having my independence but I had been involved in an accident. While driving back to my apartment after work two months earlier a HGV had jack-knifed in front of me and I was caught up in the aftermath. I remember the impact, the screech of metal against metal, an emergency response team talking to me and then waking up in a hospital. After that, the next thing I remember is waking up at my mum's house. My thoughts were fuzzy and disjointed for weeks and I suffered from horrible flashbacks. I saw the crash, my dad's funeral, my mum and my sister dressed all in black. Past relationships, enjoying good times with friends, me and my friend bringing a puppy home and naming her Mookie, past lovers, old friends I had lost contact with, then the crash again. It was always there like a weight around my neck.

When I started to feel better and my mind began to clear I would find myself looking out of this bedroom window.

Two nights ago I walked downstairs to find my mum and sister crying as they watched an old family video of us all and dad. I took a seat at the end of the couch and we all sat together in the same room and cried. The part where it was just me and Dad made me cry even more and I had to leave the room. As I reached the bottom of the stairs I could have sworn I saw him stood at the front door with that kind smile he would have on his face when we needed him most. When he smiled like that everything felt better no matter what was going on in my life. It must have been my mind playing tricks on me so I passed it off as my imagination and I ran up the stairs. The cries of sadness from the living room reached their peak as I did and I knew I had left at the right time.

As I sat and looked out of the window yesterday Jeremy, the next-door neighbour, was mowing his lawn. As I looked down the street he stood up to stretch and his eyes met mine. I was about to wave at him when he suddenly seemed shaken and visibly upset. His mouth fell open and he almost stumbled as he took a step back. He then walked away into his house while running his hands through his hair. I assume he must not have known I had moved back in and seeing me must have startled him.

Tonight I walked down the stairs and into the kitchen where my mum was stood by the cooker with a glass in her hand. I noticed a slight tremble in her hand and she looked like she was listening to try and hear something quiet.

"Mum?" I said as I placed my hand on her shoulder.

The glass fell from her hand and she screamed out loud as her eyes searched wildly around the room. Her reaction shocked me and I didn't know what to do. Was she ill? Was this a sign of some sort of Alzheimer's or the symptoms of a stroke? I ran into the hallway near the front door where she kept the house phone and there stood my dad again. I saw him this time plain as day. His smile was as plain as the nose on my face.

"Hello, Tina. You don't have to worry, it's ok," he said.

"You...you...you're dead," I said.

"I know, that's ok too," he said.

"Mum needs help. I think she is ill. You're not here for her are you?" I said.

"Your mum is fine, Tina. I'm here for you," he said.

I stood for a moment in shock, not knowing what to say.

"You're...you're here for me? But I'm ok, I…I just had an accident is all." I uttered.

"It's ok Tina. I'm here for you," he said and opened his arms to embrace me.

"But I remember being at the hospital," I said.

With a smile still on his face he looked at me in a way that was so comforting and safe.

"But I...I'm ok...aren't I?" I said.

I couldn't resist falling into a hug with him. I had missed him so much. As I did, visions of my life passed before my eyes. School, playing with friends, my first job, my first kiss, working, moving into my apartment, and the crash. The unbearable pain in my stomach and head, the doctors calling my name, the sound of a defibrillator, the darkness and silence. After a few moments I had found myself back at my mum’s house. I was looking at the hearse from the bedroom window. It was not Dad spelt out in the flowers, but my name, 'Tina'.

“I…I died?!” I said.

“Yes, love. But it is ok, you're safe now,” he said as he hugged me closer. “You're safe now.”

The room filled with an all-encompassing beautiful light and my thoughts as Tina Shibbard came to an end.

The Apartment.

I have been homeless for six years now. Some people in my situation like to stay in one place to try to get their life back together and sort stuff out. Some end up on the street for all sorts of different reasons. They're off the grid, they have a past that they don't want to return to, they feel life is better not having a mortgage, a job, bills to pay, or expectations to live up to. Then there are some like me, drifters. I get asked why I don't want a fixed abode or a place to call my own. Let me tell you after what I have seen I don't think I will ever settle down anywhere ever again. You see, there was this one place that put me off staying in one single place forever, a flat just outside Manchester city centre. It wasn't exactly mine, I had been kind of squatting there since everything went to shit, but I'm getting ahead of myself. I'll start from the beginning.

Mine was a story told thousands of times by thousands of different people. The company I worked for went into liquidation, me and all my co-workers were let go; that was it. The redundancy money was ok but it far from covered my debts and I struggled to find a new job. In a domino effect, I lost my car, my flat and my partner. Things were fragile between us anyway. Her family didn't like me and the feeling was mutual so when we lost the flat she went home. Her parents said I wasn't welcome and she didn’t even argue in my defence, so they can all go and fuck each other in their big fucking fancy house.

I knew I had to find somewhere and quick. The world is a scary place for a young woman of small stature. I used to work out and ate well before, I'm just naturally petite.

In happier times I was always playing practical jokes by hiding in a cupboard and jumping out on people. No one ever expects a fully grown woman to be able to hide inside small spaces, but thanks to some hypermobility and some training as a contortionist, it's something I can do. As a result, hide and seek is my favourite game. Something that would act in my favour in the few weeks following my life implosion.

It was early winter and a storm had settled over the city. I needed to find somewhere warm and dry. There were all these high rise flats that had been built around the city in recent years. That's where I came across Jameson Place near Piccadilly Gardens.

It was a nice looking building, all modern glass and steel but not in an office building kind of way. There had been a big, old, derelict mill here for years before the land had been reclaimed for residential housing.

So, I hung around outside and waited for someone to leave via the security door at the front of the building. As a man walked out he let the door go and I quietly slipped into the lobby before it closed. I was now in a dangerous situation. If I was caught I would be arrested and I didn't need a criminal record. I climbed the stairs acting like I knew which floor I was looking for. If I'd been going up and down the stairs for a while I would have made myself look suspicious so I exited the stairs on the second floor. I walked along the corridor searching for an empty apartment when I heard two of the residents talking.

"You hear about Callum, the bloke from 214?" said the man.

"The guy with the eviction notice?" said the woman.

"Yes. He moved out this morning. All he took with him was a bag of clothes and a few personal items," said the man.

The woman said something in reply but I was already too busy trying to find apartment 214. I saw the number on a door but kept on walking past it, through a fire door that split the corridor into two. I then sneaked into a maintenance cupboard and waited for the two people to leave. After half an hour I sneaked back to the empty apartment and got to work on the lock.

Lockpicking wasn't something I picked up since becoming homeless. There is an old warehouse near my parent's house that my friends and I used to break into at night when we were teenagers. It was a place to hang out, get drunk and you know, do things. Plus, it was warm and dry in there. Picking a lock raises less suspicion as it causes less damage than kicking in a door or breaking a window. So it's a skill we had quickly acquired.

Anyway, I had just about unlocked the door when the next-door neighbour started opening his door. He was nearly out but was distracted by a phone call and stepped back into his apartment. I opened the door, stepped inside and quietly closed it behind me.

I breathed a sigh of relief and began to walk around the apartment. The front door opened into the living area with a TV, a sofa, and a music system. There were pictures on the walls and on the far wall was a large window that looked out towards the city centre. There were two doors on the left wall and an open archway to the right that led into the kitchen. This too was fully furnished with a fridge freezer, cooker, microwave, kettle, toaster, and a foldout dining table complete with chairs. I stepped back into the living area and walked towards the two doors. I opened the one closest to the front door and found the shower room. Two bottles stood on the sink in front of the mirror, I picked them up. They were shampoo and shower gel.

"Thanks, Callum," I said quietly.

I pulled the power cord outside the shower cubical and the red light lit up.

"Yes," I said under my breath.

This meant the power was still on.

I made my way to the next door which was a bedroom with a huge king-size bed. I couldn't believe my luck. I walked back to the kitchen and began to look in the cupboards. I found half a loaf of bread, a nearly empty packet of cereal, and a jar of jam. In the freezer I found a microwaveable curry and lasagne. I cooked the curry and made jam sandwiches. It may be a strange combination but it was the best I had eaten in weeks. I went to the shower room, switched on the shower, stripped off and stepped in. The hot water against my grime caked skin felt amazing. I must have been in there for well over an hour. Now clean and fed I began to feel sleepy. I didn't put my clothes back on, I just crawled under the covers naked as nature intended and snuggled under the warm duvet. It was so comfortable, I felt like I slept for days. I woke up slowly the next day as the light of the mid-morning sun shone through the bedroom window. I wandered into the kitchen still wrapped in the duvet, grabbed the cereal then sat down on the sofa. I ate the cornflakes from the packet and watched some TV with the volume turned down low as I didn't want to alert the neighbours to my presence. Without warning the television switched off, in fact, all the electricity switched off. I sat up, being as quiet as I possibly could. I knew something was wrong and I had to leave. Leaving the duvet on the couch, I ran to the shower room, grabbed my clothes from the floor and pulled them on. I had just slid my feet into my shoes and walked into the living area when I heard voices at the front door. I stood there for what seemed like minutes but in reality, was less than a second. One thought rushed through my mind. 'Hide!'

I heard a key slide into the lock and I ran into the kitchen. The lock clicked as I vaulted up onto the kitchen counter. The front door opened and I pulled open a cupboard door that looked similar to the rest of the wall cabinets but was set into the wall. Inside I found the boiler and then my heart leapt as I noticed the tiny crawl space beyond it. I climbed in and closed the boiler cupboard door just before whoever was at the front door walked into the room.

"Ok lads, first of all, collect any of the old resident's personal items that they left behind, then we've got to clean this place top to bottom," said the voice of who I assumed was the boss.

I lay in the space and wanted to laugh so much that I had to press my hands over my mouth, I couldn't believe I had gotten away by the skin of my teeth twice in such a short space of time. I lay there in the darkness and slowly inched my way deeper into the crawl space. It wasn't really a crawl space, more like a glorified maintenance vent. I could only just squeeze my narrow shoulders in and move enough to shuffle through it. Luckily I'm not claustrophobic. My feet touched something solid, I pushed and it popped open. I shuffled down and realised it was a door that opened into the next apartment, I froze. If I was caught now the next stop for me would be a police station, but nothing happened. There were no screams, no shouts, just silence. I moved past the boiler and sat upon the edge of the cupboard doorhole. I lowered until my feet touched the counter and then climbed down to the floor. I had a look around the kitchen and then moved into the living area, all the time being extremely cautious. When I was certain there was no one home I used the toilet. I went back into the kitchen and opened the fridge. It was filled with beer, cooked meats, vegetables, yoghurts and milk. I took out some of the cooked ham, found some bread and made myself a sandwich. I looked in the cupboards and found some glasses, I took one out and filled it almost to the brim with milk. When I had finished I washed it out and put it back where I had found it. I finished my sandwich and tidied up after myself. I wandered around this apartment.

The owner had the usual type of collections; CDs, Blu-rays and books but he also had an unusual collection. On a decorative display cabinet made of shining steel and glass, he had a collection of ancient urns and vases all lit with tiny bright LED bulbs.

My dad works in the Manchester Natural History Museum specialising in ancient civilisations and cultures. When I was a kid he took me there every year in the summer holidays and taught me all about the ancient Egyptian, Greeks and Romans. So when I looked at these items I recognised some of them as Egyptian from the symbols my Dad had taught me about. The others I recognised as Greek and Roman. I had a little look, being careful not to actually touch any of them.

After a while my interest waned and I sat on the sofa to read one of the owner's books, I was about to switch the telly on when again I heard talking outside the front door. I looked at my watch, I have always had a thing about knowing the time, and it was 4.30 pm. I was back in the kitchen and climbing into the crawl space in a flash. I heard the guy come in, have a shower and make his tea. The TV came on and I could hear him talking. I assumed he was on the phone. I lay there in the confined darkness for two and a half hours until the people who were working in the other apartment finished cleaning and left. I shuffled down and climbed out back into the empty apartment.

Everything was in near darkness. Only the street lights cast a tiny amount of light into the living area. An even smaller fraction of that filtered into the kitchen. Everything had been cleaned and the smell of detergent hung heavy in the air. Any personal items that had been left in the apartment had been removed. The shower room was empty and the bed had been stripped down to the bare mattress.

"Great, fan-twatting-tastic," I muttered to myself. I lay down on the sofa and slept for about four hours. When I woke up an eerie silence shrouded the building. I got up and climbed back into the crawl space. I shuffled through and pressed my ear to the door of the next apartment. Nothing, no sound at all. I pushed the door open an inch, there was no light at all. I sat in the small door hole and used the light-up face of my watch to illuminate the room just enough to see the counter. I climbed down onto it and then down to the floor. I sneaked to the kitchen entrance and looked into the living area. The only light I could see was around the edge of the bedroom door. I watched for a few moments and it went out. I checked my watch, it was 1 am. I got a glass from the cupboard and poured myself a glass of water. There was an open packet of custard cream biscuits on the kitchen table, the type that has two rows packaged side by side. I took one out and ate it. I had not eaten a biscuit in longer than I could remember and it was gorgeous. I realised that the bloke in the bedroom might be the type that keeps a check on everything that he’s eaten and with him living alone he might know if he had left an odd or even amount of biscuits. I took another one out and ate it; purely so the rows matched you understand. I didn't move beyond the kitchen that night, I ate some more food and could hear the man snoring in his bedroom. I climbed back through the crawl space and back into the empty apartment where I curled up into the foetal position and tried to sleep. The cold from the night outside the windows was creeping through into the building. I pulled my coat tight around me but it could only keep out a small amount of the cold. I wasn't going to freeze to death, it thankfully wasn't cold enough for that. I knew that much but I was far from comfortable. After about 2 hours of shivering, I decided to climb back into the crawl space. Shuffled down till I was next to the boiler. It was warmer in there and soon I was asleep.

I was woken in the morning by the sound of a radio, Common People by Pulp drifted through the cupboard door near my head. I had to press my lips together to keep from singing along. I heard the pop of the toaster and the crackle of a knife spreading something across the toast. I drifted off back to sleep and dreamt I was dancing with the guy from the apartment whilst eating toast. When I woke up again I heard the front door lock and then silence. I stayed there for another twenty minutes before I pushed the door open slightly and peeped out. He had gone, so I sat on the edge, and then climbed down to the floor. I took the knife, spoon, plate, and cup the man had left in the drainer. I put some bread in the toaster and I made marmalade on toast and a cup of coffee. When I finished I washed the items and put them back in the drainer as I had found them. I walked to the shower room undressed and showered. I dried myself on the same towel he had used to dry himself and made sure to collect all my hair from the shower base. I'm sure he would have noticed my stray, long, dark brown hairs if I had left them. I sat on the sofa and read more of the book I had started the day before. I ate some raw carrots and some fruit and climbed back into the crawl space before he came home. I heard him make his evening meal, shower, watch TV and then go to bed. Once again I climbed out from my hiding place, ate a little and read a magazine he had bought. Once I was sure he was sound asleep I used the toilet.

These daily events began to become a routine and before I knew it I had been there for a month. I started to think of myself as his flatmate, but obviously one he knew nothing about. He paid all the bills and I looked after the apartment in the day. I think it was an even trade.

One day he came home and went through his usual routine of a meal, a shower, TV, and then to bed. When I came out of my hiding place I prepared some food and I was going to read some more of the book I had been reading when something caught my eye.

On the display cabinet stood a new urn. It was tall and bulbous around the top but became slender as it narrowed towards the base. There were markings this one the likes of which I had never seen before. They were painted on in a similar manner to the marking on the other items of pottery on the shelf, but they bore no resemblance to any ancient artwork that I knew of. They depicted a man lying down on a table, under him was a horse-drawn chariot. Beneath the chariot was a tall person with raised arms and beneath him were four smaller people who looked to be cowering or bowing down.

I approached the cabinet and looked at this urn. This close I could see it looked ancient. Even more so than all the other urns and vases in the display. I honestly only intended to look at it but I had the overwhelming urge to touch it. I reached my hand up and lightly touched my fingertip to it. That little touch was too much. To my horror, it toppled over and then rolled around in a semi-circle on the shelf towards me. It then fell off the shelf and time seemed to slow down. I tried to catch it but it seemed to avoid my outstretched hands and hit the floor where it shattered. What looked like fine, black sand was scattered in every direction across the laminate floor. I froze as the sand seemed to rise slowly into the air and swirl around me. The light in the man's room flicked on and I ran into the kitchen as I heard his door open. I heard his voice in a panicked shout from the living area.

"Oh fuck, no! No, no, no, no, no! This can't be happening!"

The kitchen was flooded with light from a single bulb that hung from the ceiling and that was it. I was caught red-handed as I stood on the counter about the climb into the crawl space. The owner, my not-flatmate, stood in the archway lit by the same light.

"Who the fuck are you! What the fuck are you doing in my apartment?!" he said.

"I'm nobody. I'm sorry I didn't mean to break the urn. I'm homeless, I've been living in the crawl space, please don't call the police," I pleaded.

“The police? The police! Do you have any idea what you have done? That urn was at least nine and a half thousand years old! Fuck, I shouldn’t even have it here. I knew I should have left it at the dig site,” he said.

As he spoke I noticed someone approach him from behind. This other person must have been in the bedroom with him. A girlfriend maybe I thought but as it got closer I noticed that the figure was growing. I also noticed that it seemed impossibly dark. The light that lit both me and my not-flatmate didn't seem to reach this other person at all. It swayed from side to side behind him in a strange, inhuman way. All the time it stood there it grew and was now huge. Nearly twice as wide as the man and when it raised its head it was taller than him by a clear foot.

Smoke began to flood around the man's feet. I pointed behind him but as I tried to scream no sound came from my throat.

“Really, you're going to try the look behind you trick? If I turned around would you have jumped into the crawlspace?” said the man.

Two huge hands wrapped their fingers around my not-flatmates shoulders.

“What the,” he said.

The man's voice was cut short as the thing sunk its teeth into the back of his head. His face twitched as he struggled, but then his mouth fell slack and his eyes rolled back in his head. His cheeks sunk in and his skin turned a pallid grey. My scream finally erupted from my mouth in an animalistic howl. The thing slung the man aside and stared directly at me. It was black in colour but the eyes were two slits of complete and utter darkness. Its mouth was a jagged hole in its face, like an endless eternal void of nothing surrounded by shards of broken glass. It swallowed all light that strayed too close. It strode towards me and let out a deep guttural hiss. I threw myself into the crawl space and dragged myself through it as fast as I could, not bothering about the amount of sound I was making. I thrust my hands out against the door, throwing it open and causing it to clatter against the wall. I grabbed the edge of the cupboard and hauled my body out of the crawlspace. As I did the beast lashed out with its clawed hand and I felt pain run from my calf to my ankle. I used my arms to protect my head and screamed as I hit the counter, then fell down onto the kitchen floor. I should have been hurt but I had far too much adrenaline rushing through my body. I stood up and looked back towards the hole in the wall. The thing's hand was clawing at wall surround the crawlspace and tearing away chunks of the tiles and plaster as it did. I hadn't noticed the commotion coming from the apartment behind me. The kitchen light was on now and I heard someone shouting behind me. The beast roared through the hole, sounding like a raging inferno. I didn't look at the couple as I barged past them and ran towards the front door but I could hear their screams as the thing tore down the wall that separated the two apartments. I fought with the door trying to get it to open but I was panicking and my brain wasn't making rational decisions. The woman ran to the door, pushed the key into the lock, twisted it and pulled open the door. I ran past her like a bullet from a gun. She should have been right behind me but when I turned to look back the thing had torn her almost in two from her shoulder to her navel and was feeding on her. It then slammed her broken body down onto the floor and ran after me.

As I ran along the corridor, a door opened and a man poked his head out.

"What's all the racket about?!" he said.

The beast charged into him, smashing him through the door frame, showering the wall, floor and ceiling with his blood. I heard another man scream in the apartment but I wasn't going to stop for anyone or anything. I made it to the stairs and ran down flight after flight as fast as my legs could carry me. How I didn't fall down every single one I will never know.

The building was in chaos by the time I got down

to the security door in the lobby. The thing was tearing the building and its residents apart and continuous screaming came from every floor. Some of the people were now coming down the stairs and scrambling towards the doors. They were covered in blood, some were missing limbs and screaming hysterically. I pressed the button to release the lock on the door and ran out into the night.

I didn't stop until I reached Piccadilly train station three streets away. A train going to Blackpool North pulled into the station and I jumped on board. As the doors closed I could hear screams echoing into the night. I have been on the run ever since.

No one seems to know what the thing is that I released unto the world that night. But at some point in the past, someone had felt the need to trap it in an urn covered in symbolic seals. They then wiped all knowledge of it from history. In my curiosity, clumsiness, and stupidity I had set it free. It has been tearing its way across the country ever since, leaving death and devastation in its wake.

As for the scratch on my leg, the wound never quite healed and the flesh around it turned as black as pitch. In the last few days, my whole leg has gone the same way and the infection is travelling further into my body. I know the thing is getting closer to me when shadow-like smoke begins to pour from the limb. I don't want to know what it will do when it finds me and I fear that I am slowly turning into whatever that thing is. If that is the case I will find a way to end my life before it's too late for me and the rest of the world. Until then I must keep running.

Atomic.

I hammered my fist against the three-inch-thick glass of the porthole.

"I'm sorry. I'm so sorry," mouthed the tear-streaked face of my neighbour, Mr Hasdale.

The four foot thick, lead-lined, plate steel door had shut and sealed itself just as I was arriving at the fallout shelter.

"You always said my lateness would be the death of me, didn't you mum," I said as I looked up at the sky.

She had died four years earlier and had been spared the agony of having to watch our once great country tear itself apart in a ferocious civil war. I never thought things would degrade so badly that nuclear war would be a reality, but sadly here we were.

I looked into the porthole again and saw that the cover had been closed on the other side of the door. As I looked into my dull reflection I saw tears well up in my eyes and roll down my face. I was doomed now and I knew it. These were my final moments.

The pale dusk air was illuminated beyond the brightest sunlight. I spun around and saw a huge mushroom cloud rising high above me. It wasn't on the horizon. It was a little over a mile away. As I watched it rise with horrified awe a deafening rumble shook the ground beneath me. Then the scalding blast wave hit me.

I was thrown against the shelter door. The heat blasted against me and everything around me burned. The steel door blackened, and were charred and torn up at their roots. Buildings burst into flames and were blasted to dust. I squeezed my eyelids shut and felt the sensation of spinning, falling, and being slammed across the ground over and over. Then everything was consumed in darkness...

A thought arose in my mind. 'Is this what death feels like? How am I thinking if I am dead?' A splinter of light broke through the darkness. As it grew I realised I was actually seeing it. My eyes were still working. I blinked and lifted my head from the ground. Somehow I was still alive. I rolled onto my back and hitched myself up onto my elbows. Every inch of my body ached and my skin was sore. I sat up and a layer of ash fell away from my chest. This dust had been my clothes. They were in the state that my body should have been. I got to my feet and swept away the remaining ash from my body. I stood there naked and pathetic but astonished. Somehow I had survived a direct hit from the most destructive weapon humans had ever invented.

I wandered around and found my car but it was an

upturned, burning wreck. I realised I had to walk home. As I walked back to town I saw the devastation that had been caused by the bomb.

Buildings I had walked and driven past most of my life had been reduced to rubble. Flames burst high into the air from a ruptured gas main. I saw water cascading down a staircase and flooding the basement of the ruins of a house.

Where people had fallen, charcoal skeletons burned on the ground. Everything was being coated in a layer of ash, dust and nuclear fallout that was now falling from the sky. I walked through the town centre. Where the town hall clock tower had stood there now lay a mass of rubble out from which the bell protruded. I continued on my way and walked through a park. The trees had been flattened and were still burning. The grass was blackened and covered with ash. The large pond had evaporated and boiled fish and frogs lay on the dry soil that had been the pond bed.

After some time I got back to the village I lived in. I found my street or what was left of it. All the way along the trek I had been foolishly hoping my house would still be there. As I got closer to it I saw the rubble and the wreckage. As I recognised items of my furniture and my belongings poking out among the debris I felt my heart drop. Everything I had ever owned, all I had ever worked for was gone.

Everyone I had ever known was now in one of the bunkers or most probably dead. I fell to my knees, and a wail came from deep within me. I cried and not even like a child. I cried like I had never cried before. I fell onto my side and curled up into a fetal position. I must have laid there for over three hours before I moved again. I heard sirens and what sounded like jet engines overhead. I looked into the sky and saw two planes chasing a long slim object. I stood up and watched them pass overhead and off into the distance. There was a flash of light many times brighter than the sun just like before then the ground shook. The blast wave rolled over the horizon and I set off running in the opposite direction. I don't know how I thought running would help but it was all I could do. I wasn't hit by the full force of it though. I turned to see it dissipating and was hit with a gust of wind so strong that it pushed me off my feet. The air was filled with dust and debris again. The planes gave me hope that someone, somewhere was still alive. I picked myself up and began to walk away in a direction away from both the explosions as I figured that direction was the most likely to have survivors. As I walked I could feel my hunger beginning to grow. I got onto a motorway lined with burnt out cars and charred bodies. There were no survivors and all the vehicles were damaged beyond use. I continued to walk until I found a sign for the next town and worked out I must have walked about four miles.

I looked around and saw the torn and twisted steel substructure of a supermarket. My stomach rumbled again and I headed in that direction.

When I got there the building, like every other in a six mile radius, was little more than rubble. I dug through it and found some cans of vegetables and corned beef. Luckily they were in the type of cans with ring pulls. I ate the food, filled a bag with cans and kept on walking.

A few hours later it was starting to get dark as the sun began to set. I knew I had to find somewhere to sleep. The further I walked the more I noticed that the buildings were more intact but there was no one here. Everyone had been evacuated before the bombs detonated. I climbed through a broken window into a house. I went into the kitchen and opened the fridge. There was a bottle of milk, a packet of sliced chicken and some vegetables. I grabbed the bottle of milk, pulled off the top and drank half of it in one long gulp. I made my way up the stairs and found the main bedroom. I realised how tired I was as I lay in the bed.

I didn't know I had fallen asleep until I found myself waking up. My entire body ached and my skin felt like someone had rubbed me all over with sandpaper. The sun shone through the window and I decided that I should get out of bed. As I stood up the skin on my right knee started to split. Blood and thick white pus ran down my shin. I stumbled down the stairs and into the bathroom. I tried to switch on the shower but there was no water so I picked a towel from the rail and cleaned my knees. I wrapped the towel around my leg and stumbled back into the kitchen to find a first aid kit but all I found were plasters. They were no use so I removed the towel and to my surprise I found that my knee was almost healed up. It was not a neat heal though, the skin was raised and tough like a callus. The left side of my head began to throb painfully. I touched it lightly with my fingertip and felt a large boil there. I quickly recoiled my hand in shock as I felt something move under the skin. I ran into the bathroom and vomited all over the toilet bowl. As I watched, the bile that had come from my stomach began to rapidly eat away at the plastic seat and the white porcelain.

"What the fuck? What the fuck?" I said aloud. Then the pain flared up in the side of my head. I looked into the mirror and raised my trembling hand to the boil above my ear. It began to split open and pus ran over my ear and down my neck. The skin of the boil slid closed then open and closed a few times. The thing within became free of pus and blood. It was glassy like a marble and all at once I realised I could see from a wider angle. I turned my head and reflected in the mirror was not a boil, but a yellow eye set into my skull. I realised I was looking into the mirror from this new eye. I screamed and stumbled back then tripped over a set of scales. I fell into the bathtub, hit my head on the tiled wall and everything went black.

It was dark by the time I came around and my head was throbbing. I climbed out of the bath and walked into the kitchen. Through the broken window, I could see the sun rising over the horizon. My body had been going through changes while I was unconscious and I had another eye on the right side of my head. My skin felt thicker and rougher and still ached. I felt movement on my sides and when I looked down there were two large lumps on either side of my body, just below my arms. I placed the palm of my hand over one of them and I could feel something solid under the skin. As I looked down at my body tears rolled down my face. And not just my face, my new eyes produced tears as well. My skin was red all over and looked inflamed and possibly infected. The lumps on my sides pulsed and moved ever so slightly.

"What is happening to me?" I sobbed.

There was no one here to hear me. As far as I knew there was no one left in the world. Just me. A useless nobody who couldn't hold down a job but had somehow managed to survive a nuclear bomb. I don't know how and I don't know why. Maybe this was just a punishment for being shit at life. I couldn't even die properly and now I was growing new body parts that I had no use for. I lay down on the floor and felt sorry for myself.

Half an hour passed and I began to feel hungry. So, I got to my feet and looked in the fridge. The chicken was out of date so I left it there and took some of the carrots and ate them as well as a can of cold hot dog sausages that I found in one of the cupboards. I opened the tumble dryer and found a pair of jeans, a hoodie, and a t-shirt. They were all a little bit too large but they were better than being naked. There was a backpack near the back door that had a pair of running trainers inside. As luck would have it they were my size so I put them on and filled the backpack with cans and bottled water then set out to walk again.

After four hours I had travelled ten miles and had still not seen another living being. I stopped near a park. The entire place was full of dead birds. They must have been flying overhead and fallen here when the bombs detonated.

I ate and drank and moved on. Without warning, a pain shot through my sides and I fell to my knees. I pulled off the hoodie and the lumps on my sides were growing. They looked like long, stubbly spikes now. With a gush of blood and puss, one on my right side forced its way out of my body. This new limb hung there limp for a moment. It then raised up towards my face and I looked at it. I realised I was moving it. It looked like a crab's leg with four points of articulation. What was I becoming?

More bombs fell that day destroying more of this once beautiful planet and further reducing my chances of finding anyone alive. One of them in the direction I was heading. I didn't know what to do so I decided to turn back.

Over the next two days new limbs burst out from the three other growths on my sides. Like the first I had complete control over these new limbs.

I was eating cold peas directly from a can when I swallowed something hard. I dropped the can and spat the peas out into my hand. Among the peas were the corroded remains of my teeth. I ran my tongue or my gums and could feel the wide, serrated edges of some new boney structure. A rage grew in me and I swung my arms out. I picked up a can of beans and threw it. I reached for another, but before I could grab it, the sharp tip of one of my new limbs was driven right through it. This stopped me in my tracks. I looked at the can with a mix of horror and awe. I held the can up infront of me, took hold of it with my hand and pulled it from the spike. I moved one of my new limbs and drew the tip across the remaining bricks of a destroyed house. It gouged out a line in the hard surface. A smile played across my face. I jabbed the tip at the bricks and punched a hole right through the wall. I swung another limb and smashed the wall, throwing bricks and mortar like it was nothing more than polystyrene blocks. After an hour of smashing everything around me I began to feel sleepy so I lay down on the ground.

I woke up the next day and couldn't move. It felt like I was trapped inside my skin. I twisted and pulled and moved. There were cracking and tearing sounds. I felt the urge to pull and break free. As I moved my head back I felt a breeze on my neck. I twisted and moved and felt the sensation of pulling a hat from my head. I opened my eyes and infront of my face was a thin pale shell. Like snakeskin and a perfect void of my head. This was skin wrapped all around me. As I writhed and wriggled until it split and came away from me. Soon I was completely free from it. My skin was light grey and softer than it had been the day before, but I now had large plates of flesh all along my limbs. The breeze felt wonderful so I stood there and let it caress my body. I noticed that the plates were hardening and becoming shell. Whatever was happening to me seemed to have some sort of purpose. I wanted to see what I looked like, so I broke into a house and climbed the stairs. In the bathroom found a huge wall-length mirror. The thing in the reflection was me, but not the me I had known for the past 32 years. I was six feet tall and still looked vaguely human but every part of me that wasn't jointed was covered in a hard exoskeleton. The incoherent rage came over me again and I thrust all four of my arms forward and smashed the mirror. I then smashed the toilet and the sink. I tore the door off its hinges and punched holes in the tiled walls. The next few minutes were a blur as I tore my way through the house. I pulled the kitchen sink off the wall, took hold of the fridge and pulled it forward to tip it over. I rammed my spikes into it and lifted it off the floor. I was shocked by my strength. I raised it above my head and slammed it against a wall. I drew it back and then threw it against the wall which gave way and the ceiling began to cave in. I turned and ran before the falling upper floor could crush me. I ran out into the street and roared in anger. I tore down ruins and smashed my way through the walls of houses. Slowly but surely I calmed down and I began to feel human again. I found my bearings and began walking. The rage that took over me was terrifying but I kind of liked it. I had spent my entire life wishing I was something more, something better, and now I was.

Five hours later I was only a few miles from what had been my home. I walked into the rubble and found some cans of food. I tore one open and guzzled and slurped at the contents without looking at the label. It felt soft and tasted sweet like fruit which made some part of my mind happy. I walked through the night and as the sun rose I was on the road that leads to the mountain the bunker was built into. A glimmer of light further up the road caught my eye and I watched as it headed in my direction. It stopped about one hundred feet away from me and two people in Haz-Mat suits with tinted visors stepped out of it. A glimmer of hope grew inside me and I ran toward them. They both turned and saw me coming.

"Help me. Please, help me!" I shouted as I ran. They both turned and ran back towards the van. I was feet away from them when one of them raised a gun.

"Wow. Calm down! My name is…"

Before I could finish my sentence they shot me three times. The bullets hit my chest but didn't pierce my shell. The anger, that animalistic rage rose in me once again and took control of my body. I stepped toward the person who had shot at me and thrust all four of my spiked arms into their torso. There was a hiss of gas as their suit was breached and I heard them try to scream. I spat at them and it as my saliva touched the suit, it hissed and ate away the plastic layers. The person's skin began to smoke as well. I watched for a moment, then wrenched my arms in different directions and tore them apart. I grabbed the van and threw it aside. The second person who had hidden behind it now stood there cowering and shaking. They stumbled back a little before I leapt on them. I slashed at the suit and tore away their mask and saw that he was a man of about the same age as me. He screamed as I pushed my spikes into his chest and lifted him up. I was then overcome with the urge to bite him. I tried to stop myself but the animal I had become was taking over. I drew back my lips and bared my new sharp teeth. I pulled this man close and bit deep into his head, slicing away the area from just above his eye to the edge of his hairline. I crunched and swallowed this chunk of him while his body convulsed and shuddered and was then still. His flesh was warm and succulent as I bit off more of him again and ate my fill. All resistance in me died and I knew then I was no longer human. I am a predator and humans are my prey.

Soon my hunger returned, I needed to eat and I knew exactly where to find enough meat to feed me for months. I made my way up the hill and approached the four foot thick, lead-lined, steel plated door. I tapped one of my spikes against it and then drew the tip across the burnt surface. With a push I forced all four of my spikes into the seal. The metal tore around the rim and I pulled. It moved a little, then there was a groan, followed by the sounds of tearing and snapping of steel. I heaved and pulled the door from its coupling and dropped it to the ground with a heavy thud. As I stepped into the bunker I could hear the chatter and cries of people who had once been my friends and neighbours. As I moved through this building, hacking at the people and feeding on their flesh, I called out for my old friend.

"Mr Hasdale, Where are you, Mr Hasdale," I called in a sing-song voice.

And then I saw him. I grabbed him, but he struggled, so I pinned him down and held his face in my hands.

"Mr Hasdale. You left me out there to die. But I didn't die, I got better. Now I'm back for you," I said.

He whined and begged for his life like all humans do, until I bit out his eye and revelled in his screams.

Confined.

He awoke this day as he did most days, lying on a cold, metal examination table. His arms and legs were strapped into place and a metal bit was strapped tightly between his teeth. His captors had found out the hard way that a seven foot tall confused man can become a tad bitey.

He wasn't awoken today by the strip lighting set into the ceiling of the operating theatre, but by a voice. It was quiet, just a rhythm in his head but it was there. The words were not clear but the voice was sweet and calming.

A sudden pain in his arm quickly brought him back to the real world. One of the small people was injecting him. He raged and fought against his bindings but the fabric held. He fought everyday but the restraints were too strong, even for him. There was no way he was going to break out but the person with the syringe stepped back all the same.

He felt his arm going numb, his vision blurred and he could feel them pulling at the skin of his forearm. He watched as they cut pieces of the muscle from his arm and cut them into smaller pieces. They put some of those pieces in test tubes, added solutions and put the test tubes into centrifuges. Other pieces they put under microscopes. They worked fast as his flesh was already beginning to heal before they had even finished.

He didn't know why they were doing this to him.

He had been here in this building for as long as he could remember. Over the years the building had changed around him but he was always there. The instruments that they used changed too. Everything now had lit up symbols that made no sense to him. He still didn't understand the language that they spoke either. The things they did to him were always the same though. Always painful, always removing parts of him. His eyes, his muscles, his limbs and his internal organs. He once had no choice but to watch as they cut open his stomach and disembowelled him for no other reason than to see what would happen. They had even removed his heart once too. The removed parts always regenerated and this seemed to be the thing that these small people were always fascinated by.

These people used to live in tribes and back then they looked up to him as a god. Bringing him food, and other offerings for him to enjoy. They knew he could destroy them if he wanted so they wanted to keep him happy and placated. These new people who were always completely covered in white clothing just seemed to want to butcher him. They weren't scared of him either.

"I'll destroy you all!" he had roared on many occasions. In reply to this, they would either ignore him or chittered back in their strange languages.

He couldn't remember his name or how they got him here. He just knew he had been here a long time.

These people finished what they were doing and all left the room. It began to fill up with the odd tasting gas that made the room spin when he breathed it in. He woke up disorientated but back in his holding cell. His arm was completely healed now. He sat up and when his vision corrected itself he stood up and stretched. He looked around him. As he did he could hear them talking and moving around outside his cell. He had stopped trying to escape long ago after he had found that the door and the walls were solid. There was no way out and even if he did get out he had no idea where he would go.

'If the world had changed as much outside as it seems to have done in this building, it is a world I don't know and won't understand,' he thought to himself.

His spirit was broken, his passion for life had gone. He merely existed in here. He lay down and stared at the ceiling. As he drifted off to sleep the singing voice grew louder in his mind again.

"Wake up, Wattok. Wake up. Stand, Wattok. Stand and fight. Freedom. Freedom. You will breathe the free air again, Wattok. You will breathe the free air and I will breathe it with you. Freedom, Wattok. Freedom," sang the voice.

He woke with a start with one word on his lips.

"Freedom," he said in a whisper.

It was a word long forgotten by him. A word he had once known but this place had driven out of him as it broke his spirit.

The voice continued to sing and it was getting louder.

"Remember who you are. You are Wattok.

Remember what you are. Remember me. My name is Aliares."

"Wattok. Aliares," he muttered.

He sat up and got back to his feet.

"Remember who you are, Wattok! Remember you were free once! You can be free again! Free!" thc voice sang.

"Wattok! Aliares! Freedom!" he roared.

His mind began to clear. The apathy and lethargy that he had been forced into began to fall away.

"Wattok will be free!" he roared.

He ran at the door and threw himself against it with all his weight. Outside he heard the little people chittering and shouting. He ran at the door and slammed against it with all his weight and this time it shifted. He hit it harder again and put a dent in it. The more he hit it the more it moved. The little people on the other side on the door were screaming in alarm. There were more voices now than he had ever heard. The gas started to flood into the room though vents in the ceiling. He hit the door again but the gas was stripping away his strength. His head was heavy and his vision began to become an array of little multi-coloured spots of light. He stumbled and fell to the floor.

"Wake up Wattok. Wake up. Stand up, Wattok! Stand and fight! Freedom. Freedom! You will breathe the free air again, Wattok! You will breathe the free air and I will breathe it with you! Freedom, Wattok! Freedom!" sang the voice over and over again in his head.

It was so close now that it was almost as if it was in

the room with him. He wanted to stand but the darkness consumed him.

He opened his eyes and blinked in the fluorescent lighting. He tested the straps and they held as they always did. One of the people walked toward him pushing a stainless steel trolley with a needle and blades all laid out on top of it. Wattok bit down as hard as he could on the bit in his mouth and cold metal shattered. He spat out the shards and the straps fell away as he shook his head. He drew in a lung full of air.

"Wattok! Aliares! Freedom!" he roared.

The little people around him began to scream and shout. He raged and fought against the straps. The one that held his left wrist started to give way and tear. The people jumped on him and tried to hold him down but he easily threw them aside.

At that moment the entire building shook with an explosion. Alarms started to wail and the people were scrabbling to get out of the room before the door slid closed and the locking bolts slid into place and sealed it. There was a cacophony of noise outside of the lab. Gunfire, explosions and screams of terror. It all began to die down as whatever was attacking them got closer to the door. There was a moment of silence then something slammed against the door repeatedly. The people stuck in the room were crying and screaming. The door started to slide open a little as one by one the locking pins broke. It then slid all the way open. A figure stood in the door way and looked directly at Wattok. The sounds of gunfire echoed around the room and bullets punched into the figure's back. They turned around and a blade split the air. The figure stepped back out the room. There were screams from several people, the sound of the blade splitting flesh and bone, then silence. The headless body of a man was thrown the doorway and across the room like a rag doll, cascading blood in all directions. It hit the floor and slid to the far wall. The figure stepped into the room after it. Their clothes were torn but still holding together enough to sufficiently cover what Wattok could see was a female form. She walked over to him and made eye contact with him. Her eyes were black, bulbous, and reflective. She reached up and removed what he would later learn are called goggles and a balaclava. She looked like the little people only taller with pure white skin and purple eyes. She smiled.

"Wattok. It's me, Aliares. I'm here to free you," she said.

She cut his bonds with her blade that still dripped with blood. He rubbed his wrists and stretched out his aching limbs.

"Aliares. I hear you in here," he said and tapped the side of his head.

"Yes, Wattok. That was me singing to you. It's taken me hundreds of years to find you. Now we're getting you out of here," she said.

She helped him to get off the table and supported him as he found his balance. One of the little people ran at them screaming in its chittering voice. Wattok slammed his fist down hard onto the person's head. Blood shot from their eyes as their skull collapsed in on itself. They fell down and didn't move again. The other people huddled in a corner and cried.

"What do you want to do to them?" said Aliares.

"Show them the same mercy they have shown me all these years," he growled.

Aliares and Wattok reached into the huddle of people and pulled individuals away from the group. They screamed and cried but Aliares and Wattok were merciless as they tore them limb from limb and left them scattered across the floors. They then killed the few remaining people as they moved through the corridors. They passed through rooms he had never seen until they arrived at the hole that had been punched in the exterior wall. As they stepped through it the air was crisp and fresh with the chill of winter. Wattok's nostrils snorted great lungfuls of the free air Aliares had promised. A large, noisy metallic object was descending towards them from the open sky above. Lights flashed across its underside, the thudding sounds it made were immense and it caused the air around them to swirl in a way Wattok had never experienced. He cowered down but Aliares took his arm reassuringly.

"Don't be afraid, Wattok. It's a helicopter. It's just my flying machine," she said.

The helicopter landed fifteen feet away from them and Aliares guided him on board.

"I'm going to help you remember who you are. I was there when they took you. I promised myself I would find you and now I have kept that promise."

she said.
She fastened his seatbelt and then fastened her own.
“Ok, Zak. Get us out of here,” she said to the pilot.
The pilot nodded and the helicopter took off and flew into the night.

Fox-proof.

When my wife Sarah and I first viewed the house at number seven East Docks Lane one of the things that really stood out was the size of the garden.

"It's eighty-six metres long and fifty-two metres wide," said the estate agent with a smug smile. "The previous owners split the garden into two distinct halves. The half that lies closest to the house has been landscaped with raised beds, a lawn, two patios and seating areas on different levels. The last forty metres have been left to grow wild. There is a low fence and beyond that it backs onto a meadow and a wooded area beyond."

Sarah and I looked at each other, I could tell she was already daydreaming of barbecues and relaxing on lazy Sunday afternoons. The house was beautiful too. A four bedroomed detached house that was a mere fifteen minute drive from both our places of work.

We had driven past a few times and had fantasised about living there, so when a wealthy great aunt of Sarah's passed away and left her a hefty sum of money in her will the house suddenly fell well within our price range.

"Let's go and view it!" Sarah had said as she grabbed my arm and grinned from ear to ear.

"Ok," I had said, unable to hold back my own smile.

After the viewing, we rang up the estate agency and put in an offer that same day. We danced around the kitchen the next day when they rang us back to say it had been accepted.

We put our old house on the market and found a buyer within two weeks. The legal documentation for the new house took three months to sort out and two weeks after that we had moved in.

The main rooms were already nicely decorated but there were some things that needed sorting out so we would do them when we got time.

A few more weeks passed and one weekend I was stood looking at the overgrown area at the far end of the garden. I was trying to picture what to do with it in my mind's eye. Sarah sneaked up behind me and grabbed my waist causing me to jump so much I nearly fell over.

"What the... You nearly gave me a heart attack!" I said.

"I'm sorry. I thought you had heard me," she said through a fit of laughter.

I took her by the waist and tickled her.

"Give over you fool," she giggled as she tried to wiggle loose.

I wrapped my arms around her and pulled her close.

"What do you want to do with this piece of land?" I said.

"Chickens," she said.

“Chickens?” I said.

“Yes. We need to have some chickens. My grandma and grandad used to keep some; they were lovely. We could rescue some ex-battery hens. There is a group that knit little jumpers for them if they have lost their feathers. I think they would be really sweet, pecking and scratching around. And when they grow their feathers back and start laying again we'll have fresh eggs every few days,” she said.

Her smile lit up her beautiful face and that’s it, I was sold.

“Ok, chickens it is,” I said.

That night I searched on the internet and found a place that sold both the chickens and the little jumpers that Sarah had spoken about. I also searched how to make a chicken run and the next day I went to a hardware store and bought the supplies I needed.

With help from my friends, Peter and Carl, I dug a hole, two feet deep, twenty feet wide, and twenty feet long. We drove the corner posts of the frame into the ground, then attached the supporting poles and a gate for access. We lined the hole and the frame with chicken wire except for the top. After that, we filled the hole with concrete and when it was dry we placed the chicken coop at the far end. We stood back and admired our handy work. When

Sarah got home from work she looked very impressed.

"Nothing can get in can it?" She asked.

"No, don't worry, it's completely fox-proof. I found out how to build it online," I said.

I was feeling rather pleased with my and my friend's work so we had a barbecue as payment for their hard work.

The next day we went to a farm we had discovered who were selling chickens for a good price. When we arrived we saw the building that housed the chickens was surrounded by violets. Hundreds of the purple flowers covered the flower beds that led towards it.

"That's a heck of a lot of violets," I said to the farmer.

"Yes, er, the chickens love them. They would eat them all day if they could," she said.

I got a distinct feeling of unease from her when she talked about the plants but passed it off as just my imagination.

We bought four chickens that day. They were all missing some feathers and as a result, looked a bit slim. They were timid on the journey home but when we finally released them into the run they all began to perk up. They seemed happy to be able to run around and peck at the food we put down for them. After some discussion between Sarah and I decided to call them Victoria, Boudicca, Cleopatra, and Helen. A few weeks went by and they had gotten used to us coming in to clean out the run, change the straw in their coop, and make sure they were healthy.

One morning I went out into the garden to check on them and there were only three. I looked around the run and found nothing. There were no signs of a scuffle, no blood, no footprints, and there was no damage to the fence. Just one less chicken. Helen had gone without a trace. I didn't know what to do and I didn't tell Sarah as I didn't want to upset her. I went about feeding the others and checked that they were ok. None of them were injured, or scared and they were fine about me being in there with them. The rest of the day passed without incident and the remaining chickens were happy. The night came and I tended to them before closing the run for the night.

The next day when I checked on them there were just two. Again, the remaining birds were fine, the fence was fine there was just one less chicken. Cleopatra had vanished so I told Sarah this time. It was a bit obvious that the number of our chickens had dropped by half.

She was upset and tears welled in her big green eyes.

“I thought you said it was fox proof!” she said.

“I did and it is. The fence is still undamaged. There are no holes, no signs of digging or anything. There are just two chickens that have vanished into thin air,” I said.

“What are we going to do?” she asked.

“I’ll tell you what I’m going to do. I’m going to sit out there tonight and watch them. If anything comes sniffing around I’ll scare it away,” I said.

“You'll do that?” she said as a little smile played across her lips.

“Yes. I’ll do whatever it takes to keep them safe,” I said.

The rest of the day whiled away and as the sun began to descend towards the horizon I took a patio chair across the garden and sat down ten feet from the run. I had an eBook to read on my phone called The Hunted and other twisted tales. Anyway that is beside the point. Every few minutes I would cast my eyes over towards the run and the coop. A few hours went by and the sky began to grow dark. Since I had sat down bats had flittered over my head as they caught flies and moths. Now I became aware that it had gone eerily quiet. My phone was set to dark mode so my eyes didn’t take long to adjust to the darkness. I looked around and was certain I saw some movement near the back of the garden. I stayed quiet and shut off my phone so I was hidden by the darkness. There was definitely something there other than me but everything just appeared as silhouettes against the night. Another hour passed and I was starting to feel tired until I could have sworn I heard a sigh. I thought it was the darkness playing tricks on my tired mind until the silence was broken by a voice.

“Are you going to leave soon? It’s just that I'm getting hungry and I feel a bit weird with you here watching me.”

It was said in a jovial way but was filled with malice.

“Who said that?!” I said as I leapt out of the chair. I looked around as my eyes searched for the source of the voice. A dark figure rose up out of the long grass. It stood seven feet tall and glistened in the moonlight. I ran at it waving a broomstick. It was then that it raised its head and the moonlight caught its deep red eyes. Its long snout pointed directly at me and as its lips pulled back from its teeth it let out a low pitched growl.

I would like to say that I roared back at it and swung the stick at its head but that is not what I did. I turned and I ran as fast as I could back into my house and I locked the door. I didn't open it again till the morning. I couldn’t sleep that night so I paced the house while Sarah slept in bed. Not wanting to wake her I sat down in the living room and eventually exhaustion pulled me into a fitful sleep.

I woke with a start and looked at my watch and saw that it was five a.m. and the sun had risen. I unlocked the door and slowly opened it. I braced my body weight against it in case whatever had been in the garden was still there and tried to get in the house. I couldn't see it and the birds were singing so I stepped outside and slowly made my way to the chicken run carefully choosing every step I took. When I got there I looked in and saw only one chicken remaining. Boudicca pecked and scratched around in the soil. She was oblivious to the fact that she was the only one left. I felt bad as I could have saved Helen but I had turned tail and ran. But what else could I have done? I had no idea what that thing was or what it was capable of doing.

I went to the shed and got the remaining chicken wire then covered the top of the run. I wired it all together and made sure that there was not a single gap. No point where anything could gain access to my lone surviving hen.

Sarah came downstairs at seven a.m. and saw me in the garden. She came out watching me still wearing her dressing gown.

"Did you stay out all night?" she said.

I looked at her and forced a smile.

“No. Something came into the garden last night. It managed to swipe a chicken before I could stop it,” I said.

“What do you mean, something?” she said.

“It must have been an owl. I didn't get a good look at it, all I know is that it was big and had wings. That’s why I'm putting the chicken wire over the top,” I said.

“What are we going to do? We only have Boudicca left, I thought this was going to be so nice but it’s all going wrong,” she said as tears welled in her eyes.

I climbed down from the ladder and pulled her close.

“It will be nice. I'm going to stay out again tonight and make sure whatever it is doesn't come back,” I said.

She smiled and hugged me tight. I put my chin on her shoulder so she didn't see the look of fear on my face.

I spent the rest of the day looking online trying to figure out what I had seen and trying to learn how to defend chickens. The only information I found was how to defend chickens from foxes; nothing more. The night came around faster than I would have liked. I picked up my chair and moved it to a different position in the garden. This time I took my trusty cricket bat. Again as the sun descended towards the horizon I sat down and waited. About half an hour passed when I saw a shadow pass over my garden. It must have been no higher than twenty feet above me.

I jumped up from my seat and looked around the garden. In the dying light, I saw a huge winged animal swoop down towards me. I froze with fear. It slammed into me, knocked me off my feet and grabbed me in its front limbs. It then crashed down onto the floor. If I hadn't seen it for myself I wouldn't have believed it. As it stood over me I could see it for what it was. Its long neck and its snout with rows of long, serrated teeth. There were two rows of horns over the crown of its skull and down its spine. Its long but strong body was covered in layers of black and purple scales. On its back, it had a pair of large leathery bat-like wings. There was no denying what I was looking at. This was a dragon.

“Do you think this is a game?” It said with its snarling jaws inches from my face.

“Wha...What do you mean?” I said.

“You know full well what I mean, the wire over the top. Are you trying to stop me or something? You don't seem to understand how this works, so, I'm going to explain it to you so you can get it through your thick skull. You may own this house but I have claimed the garden as my own. That means that everything in it is mine. The previous owner understood that. I expect you to understand too. Now, I'm going to eat the last chicken and tomorrow you are going to get me more," It said. Its teeth ground together as it spoke and its eyes burned with a deep hatred for me.

"And what if I don't?" I said with an air of foolish defiance.

"Well, then I'll eat that lovely, sweet wife of yours," It hissed.

The look of horror on my face was plain to see.

"Yes, I know about her. I have been watching you since you moved in. Now bring me more chickens or I'll suck the blood from your wife's veins and tear the flesh from her bones," It said.

With that, it jumped off me, landed on the side of the run with its hind legs and tore the top open with it's front legs. It then climbed inside and opened the top of the coop. It stuck its head into the little wooden building and, with a sharp flick of its head, grabbed Boudicca. It raised its head and looked at me dead in the eye. Without breaking eye contact it crunched the bird's body in its powerful jaws and swallowed it whole in an undeniable warning to me. I jumped up and ran at it swinging the bat over my head as it climbed out of the run. I threw the bat directly at it but it opened its mouth and blew out a blast of intense flame. The burning bat fell to the floor and I stopped in my tracks.

"Remember, more chickens tomorrow, or it will be you and your wife that I eat," it said.

It then jumped into the air, threw out its wings and flew away.

I stood there for a while mulling over my options. I didn't have much choice but I was not going to be terrorised by this thing.

I finally went back into the house and went to bed, what else could I do?

"What happened, love?" said Sarah.

"I saw the thing that has been eating our chickens," I said

"And did you chase it away?" she said.

"No. It chased me," I said.

"It chased you? What on earth was it?" she said as a look of confusion crept over her face.

The thought of telling her that a supposedly mythical beast had eaten our chickens did cross my mind. I also realised it might sound like I had lost the plot.

"It was a big owl, huge, gigantic," I said.

"Should we call pest control?" she said.

"No. No, love. I'll go back to the place where I bought them from, get some more and ask for some advice," I said.

The next day I got up, had a shower, a light

breakfast, and headed out. I arrived at the farm and walked into the farm shop. It was a small extension that had been built onto the side of the farmhouse. Inside there was a little counter from behind which they sold milk, eggs and homemade bread. As I walked in through the door a bell rang and the owner came in through a door behind the counter that led back into the farmhouse.

"Hello. How can I help you?" she said.

"Hello. I bought some chickens from here the other week and they have been attacked," I said.

"By foxes?" she said.

"Er...no. It was an animal of the winged variety," I said raising my eyebrows in emphasis.

"A bird of prey maybe, like an owl or a kestrel?" she said obviously not getting or ignoring the hint.

"No, it was much bigger and had scales," I said. She squinted her eyes and gave me a look of suspicion

"Are you taking the mick?" she said.

"No, unfortunately, I'm not," I said.

She raised part of the counter, walked past me to the door and turned the sign around to show the shop was closed to anyone else who might want to come in.

"You have a dragon problem. Yes, I know it might feel like you're going crazy but you're not. They do exist but most people never see them.

They're mostly nocturnal and they can change colour to blend into their surroundings to avoid detection. Was the one you saw about seven feet tall, with red eyes and black and purple scales?" she said.

"Yes, how do you know?" I said furrowing my brow in confusion.

"It sounds like Durook. I have had run-ins with him before. He's a nasty piece of work but quite harmless and easy to deter. Let me guess, he threatened you, maybe said he'll eat you if you don't get him more chickens," she said.

"Yes he did, he scared the crap out of me," I said.

"Take no notice of him. He's full of piss and wind. You need to plant violets. Did I not tell you that when you bought the birds?" she said.

"No," I said.

"Oh bloody hell, I am sorry. It must have slipped my mind. They're a natural dragon repellent, you see. They aren't lethal but they can't stand the smell of them or go anywhere near them. If they touch them it'll make their scales fall out. The chickens love them though, they can eat them too. That is why my chicken shed is surrounded by them. I'll give you some in pots to take with you now. If you need any more help come straight back to me," she said.

"Thank you so much," I said.

“Don’t mention it, it’s the least I can do,” she said with a warm smile.

I bought four more chickens from her that day and then went to every garden centre I could find. I bought every single violet plant I could get my hands on.

That was two years ago. These days the chickens are happy in their run and we have planted the violets all around the edge of the garden and anywhere there is space for them.

I have seen the dragon, Durook, fly past a few times since then and all he can do is snarl at me. I just give him a friendly wave and flip him the bird…so to speak.

Johnathan Valley: Number Five.

My Name is Jonathan Valley. I was born in 1983 in a little village, in Bolton, England. The only child of Tony and Beth Valley. I had always wanted to join the army, so by the age of 18 I enrolled and began my basic training. At the age of 22, I joined the S.A.S. It was around the same time that my parents died in a car crash whilst I was in active service. I threw myself into my work taking every mission I could as I felt I had nothing to come home for. Then my career in the armed forces was cut short, not by a bullet or an explosion but by a bad fall. I tore the ligaments in my left knee. I was offered an administrative desk job but that wasn't enough for me. So I retired at the age of 30 and joined the police force. I worked hard and got promoted to detective at 34. I was 37 when I became a bounty hunter IDPDA. By bounty hunter, I don't mean catching up with people who had missed court dates or skipped the country to avoid a jail sentence. I was the hunter of strange and unusual beings. I have lived a long life and had some amazing experiences. I have gained a lot of knowledge, wisdom, physical strength and ability. I have also lost a lot of friends, family, my left hand, and the freedom to speak freely.

That is why I have written the stories I present here for all to read. I suppose you could call it a near deathbed confessional. The world needs to know the truth.

For any of this to make sense I need to start at the

beginning:

I was working as a detective for the Greater Manchester Police and investigating the murders of three men. They were not the type of people you think would associate with each other. Paul Barnes was a solicitor, Jake Davies was a laboratory technician, and Colin Grace was known to the police for his involvement with the supply and transportation of drugs. Nothing class A, mainly marijuana in one form or another. They were found all in different parts of the city and apart from the fact that Barnes and Davies had been photographed on different occasions with Grace, the two men were just thought to have been acquiring narcotics from Grace.

It was 10.25pm on 27th May 2019. We had just been notified about the murder of a fourth man, Dean Simpson, who was apparently a friend of Davies. He worked as a waiter at the Little Italy restaurant. He was found in the back alley behind the restaurant where the staff went to smoke. I was questioning one of the staff members who said that she got a look at the killer.

Kelly Reynolds was twenty three, she was tall and slim with black hair cut into a bob. She was in some visible distress and trying desperately to smoke the cigarette that was perched in her trembling fingers. This is how my questioning went:

"Hello, Miss Reynolds. I'm Detective Valley. Do you mind if I call you Kelly?" I said.

She looked at me with tears running down her face.

"H-h-Hello Mr Valley. Yea, sure," she said.

"I've been informed that you saw the attack," I said.

"I saw the guy who attacked Dean. I didn't see the actual murder. I just saw the guy leaning over him. I didn't know he was…I didn't know Dean was dead," she said and tried to hold in a sob.

"What did he look like? Just try to remember for me, please," I said.

"He, er, he…This is gonna sound crazy but he looked like Dean," she said.

"You mean he looked similar to Dean?" I said.

"No, I mean he looked like Dean. Like, Identical. Like he could have been his twin," she said.

"Does he have a twin?" I said.

"No, he has a younger sister. She's about ten years younger. She's still in high school," she said.

"So Dean has a doppelganger?" I said.

"Yeah, that's it. A doppelganger," she said.

"What did you do?" I said.

"I shouted and was running over when he stood up and that's when it happened," she said.

"When what happened?" I said.

"He looked up at me and his...er...his...his face...it changed," she said.

"I beg your pardon?" I said.

"His face, it changed. I know, I know, it sounds fucking crazy. I thought I was seeing things but I swear his face changed," she said.

"Kelly, are you a user of any kind of drugs or prescription medication I should know about?" I said.

“No! No fucking way. Sir, I'm just telling you what I saw. If you're gonna start accusing me of being high or something you can just forget it. I'm tired and I’m scared,” she said.

“Kelly,” I cut her off midsentence. “Kelly, I'm not accusing you of anything. I just need to get the story right and I need to know you are a viable witness,” I said.

“Ok, I'm sorry. It just scared the shit out of me. But I’m being honest with you, the guy’s face changed. It was weird. It was like one second he was Dean the next he...just looked different,” she said.

“What happened then?” I said.

“I chased him and he ran off down in the alley,” she said.

“So, you managed to corner him at the end?” I said.

“No,” she said.

“But there’s a fifteen foot wall, it’s a dead end,” I said.

“Yep, and this guy jumped over it. He didn't climb over it, he jumped clean over it. Didn't even fucking touch the thing, so that’s when I got out my phone and rang the police,” she said.

“Can you tell me what he looked like when he changed? Could he have just looked like Dean from a side profile but looked different face on?” I said.

“No, it wasn’t like that. He and his face physically changed. Everything, his eyes, nose, his hair, and mouth; everything. He was Dean, then a moment later he wasn't,” she said.

"Ok, thank you, Kelly. Please if you remember anything else just let us know," I said and handed her my card.

"Ok thanks, erm," she said.

"Detective Jonathan Valley," I said.

"Thank you, Detective Jonathan Valley. Can I go now? I'm tired and I just really want to go and see my mum," she said.

"Yeah, sure. Just ask one of the uniformed officers to escort you off the scene. Tell them I said you can go," I said.

"Ok, thanks," she said.

"Bye," I said.

As I watched her leave I felt her statement was worthless. How the hell does a man's face just change and then he jumps clean over a wall that height? I mean come on, seriously?

I looked at the body. There was a cavity in his chest, a perfectly round hole. Something passed straight through his chest, his heart, and exiting out from his back. The other victims all had a similar wound. Cauterised with some blistering, and a completely straight trajectory. Whatever had caused it was like nothing I had ever seen. There was no haemorrhaging, no other tissue trauma and the sternum and ribs were undamaged. The exit wound was also the same size as the entry wound. It was as if something had burned a hole in him rather than physically passed through him. Like the other victims, his right eye had been removed. It was clean with no damage to the eyelid or surrounding tissue. Like it had just been popped out and removed surgically. The scene had already been swept for fingerprints, footprints, clothing fibres, etc. Not long after I had looked at it the coroner collected the body and took it to the mortuary.

I was relieved when my shift ended at 11.30 pm. I would get the coroner's report in the morning. I didn't have to attend the autopsy because it was quite clear that this was the work of the same person. If there was anything else I would hear about it tomorrow.

I drove home to my cold and empty one bedroom flat. I switched the heating on, made myself some supper, showered and slept.

I'd had a few girlfriends over the years but nothing really serious. There had just never been that special someone. I was in an extremely casual relationship with a woman named Sarah Darcy at the time but we hardly saw each other. There was nothing wrong between us. She was a lovely person and we got along fine. She was a fire officer and our working hours just made it hard for us to see each other. She had texted me saying she was working nights all week. That meant we probably would have no time to see each other again for a few weeks.

My alarm woke me at 8 am and I got up fresh and ready for the day. I had a shower, put on a clean suit then got into my old beat-up Astra and drove to work. When I got into the office I found the report on my desk. Dean Simpson's injuries were all consistent with those on the bodies of the other victims. The cause of death was the wound in his chest. The cauterization of the wound was consistent with laser burns. The only laser strong enough to burn right through a human body at that time was still being developed, it took a long time to do so, and it was huge. However, Dean's death had been instantaneous. The eye had been removed with surgical precision. Probably with an implement designed for the purpose. So we were looking for a killer who carried huge advanced weaponry and surgically precise implements around the streets of Manchester. This case was getting stranger by the day.

On our investigation board, we had photos of the victims and their murder locations but as of yet no possible suspects or leads. We thought there was a strong possibility of a drugs connection because of Colin Grace's 'occupation'. But with no solid evidence pointing to that it was just speculation.

Barry Townsend walked into my office space. He was my work colleague and a detective.

"How did it go last night? Heard you had a murderer who killed himself and then ran away," he laughed.

"Yeah, yeah. Laugh all you like, man. At least I take real cases. Lost cats aren't real cases," I said with a smirk.

He had a case a few years before looking for what he thought was a missing girl. Turns out it was a moggy with an overly eccentric owner. It's something he will never live down. Especially if he keeps going around busting other people's balls.

“Don’t worry about it. So, your witness was a junkie. It happens to the best of us,” he said, changing the subject.

“That’s the thing. She is a waitress at the restaurant and seems really straight laced. She swore she wasn't on drugs, she even became upset that I would even think she was,” I said.

“Just because she was working doesn't mean she hadn't taken something to make the shift pass a little easier,” he said.

“I know. I’m just waiting for her toxicology report to come back. This case is kicking my arse. It’s impossible for someone to carry a weaponised laser and not be noticed. I've got no suspects and the only eyewitness statement is completely fucking worthless,” I said.

“Don't worry about it. I'm sure you'll come up with something. Not all cases are straightforward,” he said.

He then slapped me on the shoulder and left me looking at the board pondering every possibility. Nothing was jumping out at me the way it did when I knew I was onto something. I looked through all the photos and was about to go for a break, then suddenly I saw someone in three of the photos. He didn't seem too important and I had never really given him much notice before but now he was jumping out at me. In one photo he was stood in the background behind Dean Simpson going into a house. In another photo he was stood next to Jake Davies on a street. In another, he was in the back of a car with Colin Grace. Maybe it was the fact he was now photographs with three of the four dead man.

"Who's that?" I said to Officer Stacy Harrison. She is a uniformed officer who was also working on the case.

"That's Eric Keane, sir. He's known to the police for some minor drugs offences but that's it. We haven't interviewed him yet as he has no set address. His sister, Janet Green, might know where he is though sir," she said.

"Do we have an address for her?" I said.

"23 Moses road, sir," she said.

"Ok. I'm going to pay her a visit," I said.

"Yes sir," she said.

With that, I left the office and drove to the address. I arrived there just after 12 pm. The house was an old terraced house with aged brickwork and hadn't been maintained for a while. The door and windows were new UPVC. The front garden was small but filled with flowers and potted plants. I knocked on the door. A Middle aged woman with mousey brown hair answered.

"Hello?" she said in a Bolton accent.

"Hello, Mrs Green. I'm Detective Valley. I'm here to ask you some questions about your brother," I said.

To which she closed the door on me. I knocked on the door again.

"Ma'am, I need to know the location of your brother. I think he may be in danger," I said

She opened the door so fast I thought I was going to fall in the house.

"That doesn't surprise me. I suppose you better come in," she said.

"Thank you," I said with a smile and stepped into the house.

The house was nicely decorated and the furniture was old but well kept.

"Please sit down," she said. It sounded more like a demand. "Do you want a cup of tea?" she said.

"Er, yes, please. Milk, two sugars," I said.

I sat down and thought about what I was going to say. Two minutes later she came in with two cups of tea. She put one down on the small table in front of me and sat down across from me.

"What is this about, Detective?" she said.

"I need to know where your brother is," I said.

"Probably out of his head with his smackhead mates," she said.

"Do you know where that is?" I said.

"No but if you find him let me know. He owes me two grand," she said and stood up.

"If that's all you came for..." she began to speak.

I quickly cut in, "Please, Mrs Green. I need to find him. Someone has been murdering his friends and associates and I think that he may be the next on the list."

"Why the hell would someone want to kill him?" she said as she sat down.

"I don't know. That's why I need to find him," I said.

"His friend, Andy Jones, lives in Farnworth. He lives at 47 Hodgend Road," she said.

"Thank you," I said.

TX I took a sip of my tea and left.

I got the address ten minutes later. The house was clearly a junkie den. The garden was little more than a rubbish tip with a few dead plants. The smell of marijuana oozed from the cracks in the walls. I banged on the door and a gaunt man opened it. He looked at me with bloodshot eyes. His stubbly beard was a result of not caring rather than intentional grooming. He was dressed in an old, moth-eaten Adidas sweat shirt and old tracksuit pants that had seen better days.

"Ello? 'Ow can I 'elp yer mate?" he said.

"Is Eric Keane here?" I said.

"Yeh. Oo wants to know?" he said.

"I'm Detective Jonathan Valley."

He tried to slam the door shut but twelve years of army and SAS training stays with you. I threw my body weight at the door. I was easily six stone heavier than this guy and I almost flattened him between the door and the wall.

"Run 'is a pig," he said.

A man in the tracksuit top and a pair of old jeans jumped up and set off running. It must have been the adrenaline because he looked like a bald Simon Pegg but ran like Usain Bolt. He must have been aware of his friend's deaths too as he decided not to use the back door but opted to jump straight through the glass kitchen window. I scaled the kitchen worktop and followed him. As I landed on the concrete floor of the backyard, my left knee twinged but I kept running. He was still going and I followed him for a mile. He was tipping over bins and all the old tricks. None of which work by the way. I kept up with him but he was not giving up. He was running through gardens and parks and he even scaled a 7 foot wall. I followed close behind but when I dropped down to the other side a pain shot through my knee. I tried to run but the best I could manage was a jog. I continued after him for about five minutes but there was no sign of him. I kept going even though I knew that there was no chance of me catching him now if he was still going at the same pace. The back streets here were a maze of tall walls that surrounded back gardens. I hoped this meant he wouldn't be able to go too fast. There was also no way I was going to leave without catching up with him.

I was jogging along when I heard his voice. He was loudly talking to someone.

"Is this some kinda joke? Oo are yoh? What do yoh want?" he said

There was no reply. I came round a corner and could see him from the left side. He was looking up another street but whoever he was talking to was obscured by a wall.

"What yoh doin' mate?" he said.

I saw a hand raise and point a small object like a thin pen at Eric.

"Wow, mate. You don't want to be pointing fings at me, man. Who do you fink you're messing wiv?" he said.

Still there was no reply. He took a step forwards with his arms held out in a threatening manner.

"Come on then ye dick'ead," he said.

There was an abrupt stop to Eric's voice as a white beam shot out of the end of the pen and passed right through him. He stood still for a second, looked down at the smouldering hole in his chest, and fell backwards in a slump. He hit the ground with a heavy, dead thump.

I stood and watched in shock as his attacker stepped into view and stood over him. I couldn't believe what I was seeing. I realised that waitress at the restaurant had been telling the truth. Now I knew why she got so defensive.

Eric Keane stood over his own lifeless body. This person looked identical to Eric but obviously couldn't have been him. Eric Keane lay on the floor and was quite clearly dead.

I pulled out my phone and rang the switchboard.

"This is Detective Valley. I need backup immediately. I'm in the back streets of..." I quickly looked around for the street signs and found one. "Back Brightfield Street."

"We have no units in your area at this moment, Detective. Please hold your position till backup arrives," said the operator.

"I can't do that. I've got a serial killer in the act. I'm gonna have to apprehend him now," I said.

"Please wait for back up Detective. Units will be there shortly," said the operator.

"I can't do that, I'll lose him," I said then ended the call and slipped the phone back into my pocket.

I was about to run out and challenge him when I was caught by a strange sense of curiosity. This thing, this doppelganger knelt down over the body.

He took a rectangular box from his pocket and placed it on the ground. The top slid open and he took out a long cylindrical tool and what looked like a magnifying glass with a thin lens. He squeezed the cylinder and four prongs extended from the end. He pushed the prongs against Eric's eye. The lids were stretched back out of the way and the prongs slid in deeper into the eye socket. The man moved the tool side to side slightly and then lifted it away from Eric's head. It held the undamaged eye in its prongs. He then held it over the magnifying glass-like device and the eye fell but it didn't hit the lens. It passed through then hung just under the device coated in a layer of what looked like vacuum formed acrylic. He took a small silver box from the larger rectangular box and placed it on the ground. The top twisted clockwise of its own volition there was a hiss and tiny jets of white gas emitted from the seal. The top then raised open and the man placed the eye into the box. The top closed, twisted anticlockwise and sealed itself. I assume this was some sort of refrigerated container to preserve the eye. He then placed all the equipment back into the rectangular box. The top slid shut, and he slipped it back into his pocket. I had watched this man be so meticulous in his method for two minutes. I knew I had to act now. I stood up and ran at him with my taser held out in front of me.

"Put your hands up. You're under arrest for the murder of Paul Barnes, Jake Davies, Colin Grace, Dean Simpson and Eric Keane. You do not have to say anything…"

I didn't get to finish the 'Rights To Silence' speech. He turned and looked at me and his eyes grew wide and his mouth fell open. He must not have been aware of my presence. His expression quickly changed to anger. It was then that it happened just like the waitress had said. His actual face changed. I almost stopped to pinch myself to make sure I wasn't dreaming. He was suddenly someone else. I didn't know what to do and I don't know why but I rushed at him. He stood up and pointed the pen thing at me and there was a flash of white light over my right shoulder. It missed my head by inches and I heard the air crackle as it passed. Before he could shoot me again I rugby tackled him to the ground. He pushed me off and stood up then raised his foot to stamp at me. I quickly aimed and shot. The taser pins stuck in his thigh and I pressed the trigger. His body became rigid and sparks flew from his chest. His flesh and muscles spasmed and flexed in a horrible jerking fashion. All areas of his body rapidly changed becoming different faces, different hands, and different clothes. His eyes watched me as I stood up. I released the trigger and he swatted the pins away like flies. His flesh continued to spasm and twitch for a moment then relaxed becoming green and smooth. His eyes became white with tiny pupils and his head looked slightly too small for his body. He had a lipless line for a mouth and no sign of a nose. He wore a close fitting bodysuit made from a black, scaled, fabric with a circuit box on the front that now emitted sparks and grey wisps of smoke. He was humanoid but clearly not human. I stood staring at him in shock as he tried to fix the circuits on his chest. He stopped and looked at me with what I assumed was anger.

"Why must you humans constantly interrupt me whilst I do my work?" he said in perfect English. Now, in the films they say things like: "You're one ugly mother fucker," or, "Welcome to earth."

"What the fuck?" was the only thing I could manage to say.

He stepped towards me and punched me heavily on the jaw. I stumbled back but caught my balance. I'd been really into boxing in my youth and in the forces. I'm proud to say I have never been knocked out. I looked right into his weird eyes.

"That all you got?" I said.

He made a noise of frustration and went to hit me again. I dodged and landed two jabs right on his noseless face. He reeled back and caught his balance. Dark green blood dribbled from his mouth. He stepped forwards and hit me but I sidestepped. I then jabbed him again and then delivered a tremendous uppercut to his jaw lifting him off the ground. He landed on his back and sat up shaking his head.

"Come on then snot face," I said.

I know it was childish but it seemed fitting at the time.

He made some weird noises, jumped to his feet and ran, but I was close behind. As he ran he worked on the circuit box on his chest. He kept changing but no form seemed to last. He ran round a corner and I followed. Ahead of us was a twelve foot wall. He leapt clean over it but I noticed there was a gate in the wall. I threw my shoulder against it, smashed through and kept chasing him. We were now within the grounds of a construction site. He was still running and I was beginning to lag behind as he turned a corner. I heard his footfalls change. As I turned the same corner a man in a hard hat and a yellow hi-vis jacket stood about ten feet ahead of me.

"Hey, you can't come in here!" he said.

I carried on running and rugby tackled this guy to the floor. I punched him twice and his face changed back into the green guy.

"I knew it was you. There is no way you could have got past anyone else," I snarled.

In one fluid movement, he stood while spinning and threw me about twenty feet. I hit the floor hard and rolled a few times. When the dizziness subsided I looked up and saw him running away in the distance. I got to my feet and stumbled trying to follow him. My legs were like jelly by this time and I cursed myself for not being in better shape. I had found what could be the discovery of the century or even the millennia. A real live alien or another highly intelligent lifeform and I had let it slip through my fingers. There was no way I was going to find him now. I ran in the direction he had gone and it led down a narrow passageway between two buildings. It was all closed in with scaffolding overhead. The passageway was about twenty feet long and stopped at a dead-end. If he had come down here he was now boxed in. I looked around but saw nothing. The passageway was empty beside a few boxes, crates, and bags of cement. The end of the passage was dark. I put my hand in my pocket and pulled out my zippo lighter. I hadn't smoked for nearly ten years but I always kept it with me as it had been handy over the years. I lit it and walked down the passage. As I reached the end the darkness felt eerie and almost tangible. I held the lighter up in front of me and moved closer to the wall raising and lowering the lighter as I went. There was a dark mass in the corner that looked unusual. As I held the lighter toward the mass it didn't reflect the light at all. I moved the flame closer and the mass backed away. Two eyes opened in the darkness then it turned back into its green humanoid form.

"Ha, got you," I said.

He replied by punching me in the face. I stumbled back as he stood up. He stepped forward and kicked me in the chest, literally knocking me through the air. I hit the ground but quickly got to my feet holding my chest. He strode towards me and I waited till he got close then threw a fast jab at him. I had caught out a few people with this in past but he dodged it quick as a flash. I threw a second but he dodged that too. I threw a third, he caught my fist mid-throw and twisted my arm up my back. He then punched me in the kidneys twice then kicked me to the floor. I began to get to my feet.

"Stay down. I warn you," he said.

Being the stubborn bastard that I am, I got up, turned and looked at him.

"Why? What are you going to do?" I said.

He came at me and I threw a punch. This one landed square in his face. He didn't even stumble, he just looked really pissed off. I threw another, which he blocked then stepped in, punched me twice in the chest and uppercutted me right on the jaw. He must have been pulling his punches before because I fell on my arse.

"Are you going to stay down?" he asked.

"No, you big green fuck," I said.

What can I say, I'm a fool.

This led to a kick in the face which broke my nose. That's why I'm so pretty these days. I fell back with the force and lay there dazed but not out.

"Stay down, you big pink fuck!" he said mocking me.

Again I tried to get up. That must have been the straw that broke the camel's back because he really lost his shit. He kicked me in the ribs and then the back of the head and down my back. He was shouting at me as he kicked me like a kickbag.

"You know how long I've been after these men?!" kick, kick. "All my life!" kick, kick. "What they would have made killed my family!" kick. "My entire fucking family!" kick, kick. "Almost my entire fucking race!" Kick, kick, kick! "Now stay down, I'm fucking warning you!" he said.

I started to move. Told you I'm stubborn.

"Yeah, why don't you just suck my big, fat…"

I felt his foot slam down on my head, my head then hit the floor, and there was a ping noise in my ears. I saw him step over me, he held one finger to his ear and his mouth moved as he spoke into some kind of communication device. I couldn't hear him as my ears were ringing. He seemed to smile at me then he turned and ran, transforming as he went. I lay there for a few minutes, bleeding and sore.

And that's when my backup arrived along with an ambulance. A paramedic ran over to me and helped me sit up. She cleaned my face up, gave me some tissue to slow the bleeding and a cold compress to take down the swelling on my face.

Stacy Harrison was talking to me as my hearing returned.

"…you ok, sir?" she said

"Besides getting my arse kicked, yeah, not too bad," I said with a stupid smile.

"Who did this to you?" she said.

"The murderer, I caught him in the act. He was using some high tech stuff. Must have been military grade. I've never seen anything like it," I said.

"What did he look like?" said Stacy.

"He was big...massive. With thick, black hair. It must have been a wig though because he had it one minute then later he was, well, he was bald. It all happened so fast. My head's still fuzzy. Can I answer your questions later?" I said.

The paramedic was wrapping a bandage around my head now.

"Yes, sir. You will have to give a full description of what occurred and a description of the murderer's appearance," she said.

"I'm fully aware of what I will have to do, Stacy, but right now I need medical attention as I may have received a concussion! I will answer all of

your questions later," I said.
I didn't like talking down to people but right at that moment I just wanted to get out of there and get treated for my injuries. Also, if I had told them what really happened, I would have been taken to a psychiatric ward for certain. They would perform a psychiatric assessment and brain scans. Both would have come back clear. What then?

"Yes sir. Very well sir," she said.
Another medic came and walked me to the ambulance.

I was taken to A&E and kept in for observation, but besides the concussion, my nose and some cuts and bruises I was fine and cleared to go home after two days.

Sarah took the night off and came round to see me. She made some food and made me sit down and rest while she cooked. I'm usually more than happy to cook. I don't like to be treated as the walking wounded but she insisted. We watched a film and talked. She tickled me a bit then hugged me when I put on the sad, gentle giant face. I asked her to stay the night and she agreed. We made love. It was a wonderful night.

I got up the next day, had a shower, got dressed with some effort and went to work. When I got in the station Barry Townsend was there to greet me.

"Chief Inspector wants to see you. Looks pissed off, man. How are you? Heard about you getting your arse kicked," he said.

"I gave as good as I got but he got the better of me," I said.

“Yes, I can see. Must have been tough son of a bitch to put you down,” he said.

“He was a fucking beast, mate. I best go, can't keep the boss waiting,” I said.

“Ok, mate. Good to see you back,” he said.

“Good to see you too, man,” I said.

I walked to the chief inspector’s office. I didn't know what to expect. Had some idiot filmed me fighting that thing on a bloody camera phone? Was he just going to say welcome back?

As I walked into the office he took a look at me and grimaced.

“Johnathan, please come in and take a seat,” he said.

Chief Inspector Wesley Spall was a tall, well-built man. He had a full head of hair that had turned grey with age. There was another man in the office too. I'd never seen him before. He was 5 feet 9 with thinning hair. He was a bit chunky around the midriff but from his build it was clear to me that he had once been in great physical shape. I walked in and sat down.

“This is Head Captain George Lawson. Head Captain this is Detective Johnathan Valley,” said Inspector Spall.

“Hello Detective. I hear you’re also from a military background too,” said Head Captain Lawson.

“Yes sir. Twelve years, sir,” I said.

“Anything you can tell me about?” he said with a smile.

Some ex-military professionals won't tell you

about their work. Some love to talk about it, and hear about it too, at any given opportunity. George Lawson was one of the latter.

"Four years regular army, three tours of Iraq, then eight years in the SAS which, obviously, I can't talk to you about," I said.

"Did you enjoy it?" he said.

"Almost every minute, sir," I said.

"That's what I like to hear, detective. Why did you opt out?" he said.

"I was out on a manoeuvre somewhere and this guy was sprayin' and prayin' with an AK47. I jumped over a wall onto what I thought was a solid roof and went straight through. I landed, my foot stayed where it was, my knee went left and the rest of me went right. Tore all the ligaments down the left side of my knee, popped my kneecap out of place, and totally messed up my day," I said.

"Ooooh! Sounds painful," he said.

"It was even more painful than it sounds, sir," I said with a grimace.

"What happened next?" he said.

"The guy with the AK found me," I said.

"Yeah?" he said enthusiastically.

"I'm here, he's not. Think that's about as much as I'm allowed to tell you, sir," I said.

"Gentlemen, sorry to interrupt but we are here for a reason," said Spall.

"Of course. Forgive me, Wesley," said Lawson.

"Sorry boss," I said.

"If you don't mind, I'm going to have to ask you to leave Chief Inspector Spall," Lawson said.

“Yes, of course,” said Spall and left the room. I had never seen him back down so easily or hand off control to anyone before. My mind began to race as I looked at this Lawson chap. Who was he?

“I had to ask Chief Inspector Spall to leave because what I am about to tell you is top secret and doesn’t leave this room. Also, Johnathan, you're off the case,” he said.

“What?! Why?! The guy kicked my arse but I will find him,” I said, pretending that I had just been in a fight with a normal man.

“No son. We know what happened the other day,” he said.

“Yes I know. It was all documented in my report,” I said.

“No, we mean we really know what really happened,” he said.

I looked down at my feet then back up at this man. I sensed I was out of my depth on this one.

“How do you know what really happened?” I said.

“Because, we have his report too,” said Spall.

I sat there for a moment trying to comprehend what I has just heard. I had that weird sensation I get when I realise things in my life are about to change. Like I’m falling through my chair.

“What do you mean his report? Whose report?” I said.

“You've only been brought into the loop because you saw him and what he can do. Do you understand?” said Lawson.

I hesitated for a moment before I spoke.

“Yes, sir. I understand,” I said.

“I was testing you before when I asked you about your military experience. Seeing if you are where the type to embellish a story. But have proved you can keep your mouth shut about things you’re not allowed to talk about,” said Lawson.

“With all due respect, sir, I wouldn't have made it this far if I was a chatterbox,” I said.

“Exactly. Now here’s the thing, the killer is not a serial killer. We made that up as a cover story. The media and the public start sticking their noses in if bodies just start turning up in random places. As you saw the individual you encountered is also not human. Or even from this planet or this time. They’re from the exoplanet Gliese 667Cc, which he and his people call Yissact. They are a species of multicellular transmogrifying organisms, shapeshifters in layman’s terms. Each of their cells is an individually functioning organism but they work together as one single organism with one collective consciousness. As a result, they can form any shape they desire which is what you witnessed. They call themselves the Omnee. The individual you encountered is named Yarhobek. He was hired by the Intergalactic Law Enforcement group as a future realignment agent. Meaning if something goes horribly wrong he’s sent into the past to put it right. Humans made first contact with intelligent, non-terrestrial life through our ancient civilisations about thirty thousand years ago. They didn't come here to invade us, they came to help our ancestral civilisations get to their feet. We didn't encounter the Omnee till about fifteen years ago. We traded with them and they took a liking to some of the plants that grow on this planet; namely Marijuana. It affects them in a similar way that it does us and is no more addictive to them than it is to us. Their cells constantly renew and regulate themselves. As a result, they don't suffer from any forms of cancer. Their bones and flesh heal almost instantly and they don’t scar. The group of men that Yarhobek was hunting were bio-engineering a strain of Marijuana that could not be detected in human blood and gave the same high but had none of the side effects. It works fine on humans but the Omnee weren't so lucky. To them it was highly addictive. It poisoned their cells and stopped them regenerating correctly. In the cells of heavy users the entire victim’s body began to mutate and the individual cells separated. They acted in a similar manner to an airborn virus, turning the cells of every lifeform they came into contact with into copies of themselves. With trillions of cells from each victim, it spread like wildfire. Other races from nearby planets tried to help treat this virus but it could mutate to defend itself in minutes. All biological life on Yissact fell victim to this virus. Then it began to cross to non-Yissact species. The virus quickly became an interstellar pandemic. Able to disguise itself as normal cells of its host, it was almost undetectable until the host fell ill. By that time it was too late. The galactic council appealed to us for the right to let the future realignment agent, Yarhobek, assassinate the five humans responsible for creating the initial drug. Five lives to save the lives of trillions. The virus had the potential to wipe out all life in the universe. We would have been killing ourselves if we had said no so obviously we agreed. Are you following all of this?" said Lawson.

"Yes. It's a bit more than I expected but I follow you," I said.

"Good. Bet you're wondering what all this has to do with you," said Lawson.

"That would have been my next question," I said.

"Well, obviously I wouldn't be telling you all this if you didn't need to know. You're just a detective. No offence," said Lawson.

I waved my hand to show there was none taken.

"The fact is we think you could be so much more. You're ex-S.A.S. You're wasted in this job. Yarhobek saw something in you. You figured out their next target, then hunted the target down even though you were injured. You fought against a being from another planet without hesitating and didn't give up even when most would have admitted defeat. He's been doing this job for twenty-seven years and said he's never fought anything as relentless as you," said Lawson.

"Really?" I said.

"Really. The point of this meeting is there is a position available as an Earth bound bounty hunter for the Intergalactic Dangerous Persons Detainment Agency. There are some sacrifices that you will need to make but the salary is substantial and there are vast opportunities for upward progression," he said.

"What are these sacrifices you speak of?" I said.

"You can never tell anyone what you do, about any of the cases you have worked or any of the threats that may be posed to national or global security. And there will be threats. This is a top secret department dealing in intergalactic secrets. Exposure of said secrets with be dealt with by the intergalactic judicial system. If found guilty you will be taken off planet and will never return to Earth," he said it just like that, plain as day.

"That's a pretty severe sacrifice," I said.

"I know, son. But this is like no job you will have ever done in your life before. It will call upon all the skills you have acquired in all your years of training," he said.

I sat forward and looked at the floor for a moment, deep in thought.

"We could give you a few days to think about it if you want," he said.

After thinking for about two minutes I looked at him.

"I have no family. I hardly have time for relationships and since leaving the SAS I have built only a few casual friendships. What can I say, where do I sign?" I said.

He looked at me and smiled. To my surprise, he produced some papers from his briefcase. I took them from him, read them thoroughly and then signed on the dotted line.

"What now?" I said.

"Make your excuses, say you still don't feel well and need another few days off. Go home, get your affairs in order and then drive to this address. You'll meet someone who you know there," he said and handed me a card with the address: 114 West Field Industrial Estate, Manchester. MH4 6JU.

"Ok sir. Thank you very much," I said.

"Thank you too, son. You've made the right decision," he said.

I stood and shook his hand and walked back to my office. Wesley Spall was waiting outside and I walked up to him.

"I still feel a bit unwell sir. I think I need a few more days off," I said.

"Yes, that is ok Detective Valley. Hope you get well soon," he said as he shook my hand and smiled.

We both knew by this we meant goodbye; I could see it in his eyes.

I collected some of my things from the office and then left via the back door to avoid seeing anyone else who worked there as I left.

I spent a day sorting out my affairs as I had been told to. Two days resting, working out, and catching up on TV shows. On the fourth day, I got in my car, typed the address into my sat-nav and followed the directions across Manchester to an industrial estate. It was fenced off with a guard at the gate. He was dressed as a run of the mill guard but I could tell in his posture that he was better trained than that. It was obvious to the trained eye. I stopped and wound down my window.

"I'm Detective Jonathan Valley. Head Captain George Lawson sent me," I said.

"Do you have any ID?" he said.

I passed him my detective badge. He looked at it and passed it back to me.

"Ok, sir. They're expecting you in Unit 4, on the left. I drove to the unit, parked my car in one of the parking spaces, and walked to the building. The door was opened before I could knock on it. In front of me stood a tall man with long hair that was tied back in a ponytail.

"Come in please, Mr Valley. Head Captain Lawson told us to expect you. Are you ready to change your life?" he said.

"Yes, I'm ready for this. I look forward to the challenge," I said.

"Are you nervous?" he said.

"A little," I said.

"Maybe this face will be more calming for you," he said.

He pulled his hair out of the ponytail and shook his head. The hair fell down around his shoulders, and then retracted back into his scalp. This man who had just been a stranger to me now looked like Barry Townsend.

"Oh shit," I said without thinking. "Sorry, I mean, I assume you're Yarhobek, right? Please excuse my reaction. Last time I met you, you were kicking the shit out of me," I said.

"Yes, I'm Yarhobek. Sorry about your nose, it was nothing personal. I just couldn't let you stop me. I assume that Head Captain Lawson has told you what I was doing," he said.

"Yes, he told me. I'm really sorry to hear what happened to your planet," I said.

As we walked through the building he turned into his real self. He looked into my eyes and smiled.

"Yes, it was a tragedy but it doesn't happen anymore," he said.

"What will happen now? Shouldn't the memory of it not exist anymore?" I said.

"It's different for different people of different species. For some, the memories are erased instantly. For others, it will fade like an old memory. For some, it will seem like remnants of a bad dream. Then there are some who live across all dimensions and see all possible timelines playing out simultaneously," he said.

A confused frown played across my face.

"I know that feeling," he said with a smile. "It's hard getting used to the fact that there are people unlike ourselves for the first time isn't it. You will learn all about the multitudes of extra-terrestrial species though."

"It seems I have a lot to learn," I said with a smile.

"Oh, like you won't believe," he said and placed a hand on my shoulder.

"How does the memory feel for you?" I said.

"It's like an old memory. It was pretty traumatic as it happened to my people and I watched the whole thing unfold. It's reluctantly holding on in here, though, it's easier to deal with than it was," he said.

"What will you do now? I mean, are you going to retire or get straight back on the horse?" I said.

"Retire? No, not yet. We Yissact don't start to show old age until at least four hundred of your Earth years. I'm only one hundred and fifteen. I still have many years left in me yet. I have a few months of accrued leave so I'm gonna go home and see my family. I remember them but it feels like I've not seen them in years. That's where the old memory thing comes in. I have this fear that they are all going to be ill like last time I saw them but I know that they will be fine. In time people will forget what I did, but that’s ok. I have my people back now,” he said.

“I hope you have a good time when you get home then,” I said.

“Thank you, Johnathan,” he said with a smile.

We reached a large office.

“You'll find Head Captain Lawson in here,” he said.

“Ok thank you, Yarhobek. Can I just ask you one thing?” I said.

“Yes. What do you want to know?” he said.

“The thing you dropped the eyes through. What was that?” I said.

“It’s to confirm the target has been eliminated. I already know the target is correct before I attack and the eye is a tissue record for confirmation if any is needed at a later date. I'm dealing with people’s lives. I can't be wrong or proven to be wrong,” he said.

“Why do you use the laser?” I said.

“It’s quick, clean, and painless. I don't like my targets to suffer. The quicker, cleaner and less painful the better it is for all involved. I didn’t want to have to kill those men, nor did I enjoy it, but the consequences if I hadn’t would have been too horrific to bear,” he said.

There was an honour in what he did. It wasn't the nicest job in the universe but he took pride in knowing that there was no vengeance or spite in the way he worked.

"Thank you, Yarhobek," I said.

"See you around, Johnathan. Maybe we could spar next time we meet. Exchange some fighting skills," he said.

"Yes, that will be good. See you around," I said. I walked through the door into the office where Head Captain George Lawson stood and into my new job and new life.

Johnathan Valley: Dead Blood.

Outbreaks of zombification are rare but they happen more than you might expect. When an outbreak does happen we at the IDPDA take it very seriously. What can start out as an individual case can become a full horde situation in a very short space of time. What most people don't know is if you get bitten by one of the infected you don't die straight away. In Stage 1 there is a gestation period of one to six hours. During this time the infection makes you become uncharacteristically violent and start attacking people. At this stage it can be cured, when the victim dies and enters Stage 2, then the real trouble starts. The infection can spread through bites and bodily fluids during both stages, though it is a lot more hazardous during Stage 2. After death, there is no cure. The only option available is elimination, as in the destruction of the brain or detaching it from the body.

One case that will always stick with me is the Wigan Infirmary case. Head Captain George Lawson approached me with a file and held it out to me.

"Jonathan, I want you to take this case. One Dr Green from the Royal Albert Edward Infirmary in Wigan called it in just now. They've got a John Doe brought in during the early hours. He was unconscious and suffering from suspected acid burns to his face and arms. They treated his injuries and put him under observation. Anyway, about half an hour ago he woke up and started tearing at the bandages. He bit three nurses and escaped through a top floor window. All three nurses have been treated but are very ill and he is nowhere to be found."

"Do we have any more information about why he was admitted in the first place?" I said.

"No. but it's now being treated as a possible first stage Postmortem Necrotic Reanimation Disease," he said.

"Man, not zombies. I fucking hate zombies," I said.

The look on his face told me the feeling was mutual.

"I know, they're horrible smelly fuckers but I need to give this case to someone. You have the experience and training required to deal with this situation, so I'm putting you on the case. It's timesensitive, I want you to get down there, find him and kill him before he infects anyone else," he said.

"How does a zombie escape out of a 3rd floor window and vanish?" I said.

"That is exactly what I need you to find out. Get

on it, the clock is ticking," he said.

I left the office, got in my Land Rover Discovery and started the engine. I opened the case file, found the coordinates and keyed them into the dash mounted sat-nav. It took a few moments to find the route and then brought up the location and approximate arrival time. I pressed start on the screen and set off. The IDPDA are not the police so we can't just put on the blues and twos to make a way through the traffic. I have to use back roads and shortcuts where I can.

I arrived at the hospital and went in search of Dr Green. I approached the reception and spoke to the receptionist.

"Hello. I'm here to see Dr. Green. Could you tell me where they are?" I said,

"She's in isolation. Go up to the third floor, then all the way to the end of the corridor and it's on the left," he said.

"Thank you," I said and followed his directions. I found the doctor by the bedside of one of the nurses.

"Hello, Dr. Green. I'm Mr. V from IDPDA," I said.

"Hello Mr. V. Thank you for arriving so fast," she said.

"This is one of the nurses who was attacked?" I

said,

"Yes. Nurse Claire Jones," she said.

"How is she doing?" I said.

"She is in a stable condition but she is still in a bad way," she said.

From looking at her I could see that her skin was pale and her breathing was shallow. Her eyes had sunken and her fingertips were dying due to her circulation being compromised.

"She has all the signs of early PNRD but she is also displaying some odd symptoms that aren't associated with that disease," she said.

"Like what?" I said.

The doctor placed her finger on the nurse's upper lip and lifted it away from her teeth. Her gums were pale and her teeth especially the canines had grown longer and become pointed.

"PNRD doesn't do this to the mouth. The teeth don't change at all at any stage of zombification. There is this too," she said.

Dr Green took a small torch from her pocket and shone a beam of UV light onto Claire's hand. The skin blistered and began to smoulder. Dr Green switched off the torch and the skin slowly began to heal.

"Photosensitivity isn't a symptom of PNRD. If this was a case of PNRD she would be awake and highly aggressive. The fact that she seems almost comatose without sedation tells me that this is something else. If I'm not mistaken I would say she has a form of haemoglobin dependant cellular mutation. Her body seems to be struggling to keep her alive while she goes through the transformation," she said.

"Vampirism. Are you sure, Doc?" I said.

"It's the assumption that I have come to. Vampirism kills the host but the transition between human and vampire is seamless so the host seems to continue to live. Whereas with zombification the host is quite clearly dead. I think this is a hindered form of vampirism as the host, here being Nurse Jones, is neither being killed nor saved by the disease. We are keeping her and the other bite victims under close observation. If they don't respond to the treatment we may need your help here too," she said.

"You said in the report that the carrier jumped out of a third floor window. That sounds like something other than PNRD to me too. A zombie couldn't fall from that without breaking bones and possibly being killed. Can you tell me where he went after that?" I said.

"That's true. Come with me and I'll show you the window he jumped through," she said.

I followed her across the ward to a window that had already been replaced.

"There is a strict protocol we have to follow. Some of the illnesses we treat here need to be contained. Any breach has to be dealt with ASAP. We can't just leave them open. I want to point out that these windows are triple hardened glass. There is no way a human could have broken through it," she said.

Dr Green looked out of the window and pointed to a large grassy area across the road from the back of the hospital.

"He ran over there and into the old derelict buildings. If he is a vampire he will have had to find a place to hide as the sun was just rising when he escaped. My money is on him being in there somewhere," she said.

"Ok, I'll go in there and find him while he is contained by the sunlight," I said.

"You should be careful. It's a hangout for dropouts and addicts," she said.

"Junkies don't scare me. The things that prey on them are what you have to watch out for," I said.

"Exactly, there could be things in there worse than vampires and zombies," she said.

"Don't worry about me. Supernatural beings are my bread and butter. Can you give me a description of the carrier?" I said.

"He was 5 feet 9 inches tall, slim build and had a bald head. He had a long nose and a wide mouth.

He still had some burn scarring when he escaped. He may have healed somewhat more since then," she said.

"So, pretty much like a junkie in a place full of junkies?" I said, not even trying to hide my sarcasm.

Dr Green fixed me with a look that told me she wasn't in the mood for such flippancy.

"He doesn't move like a human, drug addicted or not. You'll know him when you see him," she said.

"Ok, I'll get my equipment from the car. I'll report my findings back to you later," I said and took that as my cue to leave.

I walked back to the car park and opened the boot of my vehicle. I unlocked the gun locker that was concealed in the floor of the boot and lifted the lid. I took my gun belt and strapped it around my waist. Then put my bandolier over my shoulder and tightened it to my chest. I took my Desert Eagle and slid it into the hip holster that hung from the belt. I slid my Colt 1911 into my side holster and six barbed silver stakes into the loops in the bandolier. I slid my machete into the sheath on the belt. I took my AA12 automatic shotgun and slung it over my shoulder. I then pulled on my coat over all my weapons and hoisted a backpack full of silver coated ammunition in magazines and equipment up and onto my other shoulder. I closed the boot and made my way towards the derelict buildings.

Every wall was covered in graffiti and the floors were covered in litter. I took my time finding my way in there. Both vampires and junkies can get a bit twitchy when you sneak up on them.

The smell of human faeces hit me in the face like a hammer. The walls were damp and mould climbed across almost every surface. This whole place was putrid. I took my time walking down the corridors and checking every room. Most of the doors were missing or off their hinges and the windows were broken. There was very little in the way of furniture, what was left was broken and water damaged. When places like this are abandoned looters go through them like vultures picking a carcass clean.

After two hours I had swept the entire building and the place was empty. This was unusual. In a big building like this there should have been at least a handful of homeless people or addicts. They group together for warmth and safety but there was no one. I was about to give up and move on to another building when I noticed a pile of plywood in the far corner of the last room I entered and had thought I had cleared. The bottom sheet of wood was flush against the floor but I had to look. I couldn't leave without checking. So, I bent down, hooked my fingers under the edge of the board, and lifted it. My curiosity paid off. Under the plywood was a flight of stairs. I descended the stairs and opened a door at the bottom. It led to a basement in which the air was thick with the sickly smell of the newly dead. I switched on my torch and ventured further into the room beyond. There were torn clothes and shoes strewn all over the place. Personal items too including phones, keys, wallets and backpacks littered the floor. Eventually, I found the source of the stench. As the corridor widened into a maintenance room, there in the far corner, stood a pile of at least fifteen bodies. I opened my bag, pulled on a pair of latex gloves and examined the bodies. Every single body had identical wounds on their necks. There were no other injuries on them some besides some defence wounds and those caused by flies and insects that were already feasting on them. It was very clear that these were the victims of a vampire. I was removing the gloves when something grabbed me by the shoulder and threw me across the room. I hit the floor then partially slid and partially rolled to the far wall. I sprang to my feet as fast as my body would allow and in the same motion drew the colt from my side holster. I caught the fleeting glimpse of a humanoid clad in torn up bandages that trailed out behind it. It flitted across the room only stopping for a millisecond to check where I was. Then it flew right at me, hitting me square in the chest. It knocked the wind out of me but somehow I managed to catch the bandages that hung from its arm. My weight slowed it down just enough for me to aim and shoot at it twice. The bullets hit it in the thigh and abdomen. It stopped and turned to look at me. It walked back towards me as a low pitched hiss rattled from between its teeth. I had my gun raised as I tried to scramble away and catch my breath. Ash poured from the wounds in its body like the contents from a punctured sandbag. Its flow slowed as the wounds quickly healed. I've seen vampire blood turn to ash after it had left their body but I’ve never seen them bleed ash. I pulled the trigger and shot this thing in the face. As its head flew back I rolled away. It turned and looked at me as I holstered my Colt then swung the shotgun up from my shoulder. I aimed, and pulled the trigger but it moved to the left faster than my eyes could register. To my mind, it seemed to vanish then reappeared to my left. I aimed and squeezed the trigger. It shifted to my right but closer this time. I aimed at it again anticipating it to move to the left. I moved as fast as I could. As I expected, it moved to my left. I squeezed the trigger but missed it as my aim was slightly out. Most of the silver shot went over its left shoulder but some tore into the left side of its face. It screamed and clawed at its flesh desperate to remove the tiny burning balls of metal. As it did I stepped forwards and brought the butt of the gun up into its chin with a crunch. Teeth flew from its mouth as it fell back and stumbled as if it would fall. I drew a stake from my belt but it moved and disappeared. I stepped back to the wall and was expecting an attack but it never came. I picked up my bag and sneaked through this basement that now felt even less safe than it had when I first came down here. I was alone with a creature that bled ash, I had no idea what else it might be capable of.

I systematically swept the rooms down here as I had upstairs. It couldn't go outside yet so it had to still be down here. I had to find it before the sun went down or my job would become a hell of a lot more difficult. As I made my searches I walked into a long narrow room in the east wing. Under a flight of stairs I found a small door that appeared to be nothing more than a broom cupboard. I opened it and found a narrow flight of stairs that led into a sub-basement laid out as a series of tunnels. As I moved through them, I found that some were large enough for a man to stand up in and walk through while others were so narrow only a rat could squeeze through them. I opened my bag and took out a set of incendiary traps. I set one at the mouth of each tunnel. They are a canister that squirts a jet of sticky, flammable gel and are triggered by a heat enabled motion sensor. We use them to eliminate problematic vampires and are fatal to them on account that their flesh is naturally flammable. I had just positioned the trap so it pointed into the centre of a large tunnel mouth. I was setting motion sensor when the thing jumped out and lunged at me. It got a good squirt of the gel all over its back but I hadn't had time to light the ignition flame. It picked me up by the throat before I could move, squeezed my trachea shut and roared in my face. I fought for breath as I tried to hold myself up by wrapping my fingers around its forearm. All I could manage was a tiny whistle of air into my lungs. There was no point trying to loosen its grip; it was unimaginably strong. Acting against instinct, I let go of its arm then whilst I was dangling from its hand by my throat I pulled two of the silver stakes from my bandolier and drove one into each side of its chest with all my strength. The scream that burst from its throat made my ears ring and it dropped me. I lay on my side holding my throat and wheezing as I drew in deep breaths of the foul air into my burning lungs. I didn't care that it stunk like arse, it was breathable. The monster staggered around and clawed at the stakes in the sides of its torso. I sat up, pulled my desert eagle from its holster, and shot at it. Two bullets hit the thing twice in its back before it started to dodge them. It dug its fingers into its skin, around the one of the stakes, and pulled it. The skin of its fingers hissed as the silver burned into its flesh. The barbs held it in place so the thing pulled harder. As the stake came loose it tore lumps of flesh with it and the thing screamed in pain. Ash sprung from the wound and it dropped the stake. With a metallic clang it bounced across the stone floor. The thing scurried up the wall while it still pulled at the other stake as it climbed. I aimed at it and squeezed the trigger again but it dodged every bullet. It managed to tear out the other stake and cast it aside. It reached the ceiling and crawled along hugging its body to the surface like a gecko. I got to my feet and chased it as it ran. I had never seen a thing of that size move in such a peculiar way. As I chased it back up the stairs and through the basement I realised it was making its way to the entrance. The fact that it was still daylight out there proved that it was desperate to get away from me. Still I tried to keep up with it as it threw aside the sheet of plywood that covered the hole. It clattered against the wall across the room and the sound echoed through the hollow shell of the building. Sunlight and fresh air swirled into the tunnel, it was sweet and cool compared to the hot and fetid air down in the basement. The thing shrieked as it ran out into the daylight. I was close behind but it was already gone.

The sweat on my skin drew the heat from my body as I stood in the cool air and decided what my next move should be. I had to search again for the beast, there was no doubt about that. The midday sun would limit its options dramatically so it would be easier this time round. I began to sweep every room again. I dismissed the ones that were heavily bathed in sunlight. Eventually, I found myself on the upper floor that was more shaded than the lower ones. I listened but the only sounds I could hear were the soles of my boots as they crunched the dust and grit against the rough concrete floors. A shrill howl cut through near silence of the building and I'm not embarrassed to admit that it made me jump. I stood still as a rock and listened for another sound in the hope that I could maybe figure out the direction it had come from. I kept my feet planted and turned my torso and listened for something that might give me some idea of its location. Again the howl broke the silence and I was on it straight away. It had come from the floor I was on but farther down the corridor. I moved fast and quietly with all my senses on high alert. It was then that I noticed the smell, forgive the mental imagery but if you like to cook alfresco in the summer months you will know the smell of barbecued meat. That is the exact smell and it drew me to a room at the end of the corridor. It was dark inside and my eyes took a few moments to adjust after the bright midday sun. I could hear it scraping its limbs across the concrete floor. As my eyes adjusted I could make out a pathetic humanoid shape writhing in agony. I switched on the torch at the end of my shotgun barrel as I didn't want this thing to get the drop on me again. The beam of light fell upon the creature and it held out a raised palm in my direction. The light cast over a face that was charred across the whole right side. The eye was dry and shrivelled in its socket and clear liquid oozed from it. The other eye looked at me in a state of terror. As a tear rolled down its face its lips trembled and spoke a word that reached down to a humanity in me that I thought I had buried under a concrete slab of training.

"Please," it said.

The voice was hoarse but also that of a young man, and filled with a fear and sadness that I have felt myself on a few occasions. The fear of death. I lowered my gun.

"What the hell are you, son?" I said.

"I'm Danny Longridge and I'm…erm…I'm a vampire. At least, that is what I was told I would become," he said.

His voice broke and he whimpered and turned his face away from me.

"Well, either somebody's lied to you or

something has gone terribly wrong," I said.

"Yep, story of my life," he said.

He tried to force a smile but his lips quivered and tears rolled down his face.

"What happened? How did you end up like this?" I said.

He told me his story and I listened.

"I was diagnosed with tumours in my lungs, heart, liver, pancreas, and like some kind of twisted icing on the cake, one in my brain that was inoperable. All malignant too just to make sure, you know, that I was truly fucked. I had chemotherapy and was taking a list of meds the length of my arm. My family were scouring the internet for some kind of miracle cure, but obviously, there was none. Until one day my friend, Lucas, texted me to say that he might have found 'the cure'. I didn't have any time to waste so that night he came round and picked me up. We are, well, were, in a black metal band together, Vampiric Skeleton, and we had both gotten into vampire lore and culture. I thought that it was all just roleplaying and people wishing they were such things. He got deeper into it than me and took it a lot more seriously. He's a member of some websites and had started talking to people on this weird forum. Someone told him about a website that wasn't on any search engine, you had to be invited to it by someone who was already a member. Rumours said that it is run by real vampires. He had talked to someone about me, they told him that they knew someone who could help. They gave him directions to the place that he was driving me to. He parked up outside this building. It was a big, old cotton mill. All the windows were broken or boarded up and the brickwork was all decayed, and covered in moss. We got out of the car and he walked to the tall steel door, he knocked, and it was opened a really, tall skinny man with pale skin. He was wearing a hoody that had seen better days, grey cargo pants that had been black many years ago and a pair of worn out old boots.

'What the fuck do you want?' This lurch of a guy said.

'I'm here to see Val. Hellfang242 told me about this place,' said Lucas.

'Password?' this guy says.

'Lemon drizzle,' says Luc.

'Oh, ok. I'm Val, you must be Lucas Daly. Come on in,' said the man.

He opened the door wider and let us in.

He led us into a room about the size of a tennis court. There was a table about ten feet from the far end of the room and beyond that a wide, black, velvet curtain. On the table sat a notepad and a laptop. A woman sat at the table filing her nails into claws. Beside that the room was bare. She looked like she had jumped right out of a vampire movie. Long black hair, multiple facial piercings, wearing a black corset top, black pants and big, leather boots. She looked up at us and smiled. Showing off what I thought, at the time, were pointed crowns on her canine teeth.

'Hello Lucas we are expecting you. I'm Tracy. Is this your friend Danny?' she said.

'Yes,' he said.

'Ok. You know what we're doing here Danny?' she said.

'No. Luc just said he's been told that you have a cure,' I said.

'That's right,' the smile fell from her face and she took on a serious expression. 'I'm gonna be straight with you Danny, we're vampires. We can turn you, it will be a little painful at first but it will destroy all the cancer cells in your body. You will be cured, but this will be a permanent transformation. You can't turn back into a human once this is done,' she said.

'Vampires, for real?' I said with a smile.

'Yes Danny, real vampires. This is serious. Do you understand what I just told you?' she said.

'Yes. Yes, I understand,' I said.

'Ok, so the price is £1000 cash, please.' she said with a sweet smile.

'I've not got that kind of money,' I began to say

when Luc pulled this big roll of cash and handed it to her.
'£1000 cash. All used £20 notes. Will that do?' he said.
She slipped the rubber band off it and let it unroll in her hands. Her eyes were, like, hard focused on the numbers in the corner as they sprung open. 'Yep, all there. A pleasure doing business with you gents,' she said.
She had counted it all in that split second.
'If you could please go behind the curtain, Ghast is waiting for you,' she said.
'Thanks,' I said.
'See you later,' she said and winked at me as we walked across the room.
'She's fuckin' hot for you man,' whispered Luc as he thumped his fist against my shoulder..
'As if, anyway, fucking never mind that. How the fuck can you just throw down a grand like that? You can't afford that!' I said.
'Because, man, you're my friend and I don't want you to fuckin' die, ok,' he said.
'But where did you get the money?' I said.
'I sold some of my guitars, some peddles and an amp,' he said.
'Seriously? Aw fuck, man,' I said.
I grabbed him and hugged him tight as tears welled in my eyes. I knew those instruments and

equipment were some of the most important things in his life.

'We won't have as much choice instrumentally for the next few months, maybe years, but you'll still be alive, man. That's what really matters,' he said.

I cried and he slapped me on the back and hugged me.

'Thanks, man. I don't know how I will ever repay you,' I said.

'You can start by buying me some new equipment when we're rich, man,' he said and laughed.

We got to the curtain and stepped behind it. There was a guy behind there looked like a generic metalhead. Big, with black hair, black clothes and covered in tattoos.

'Danny, Lucas. Hello, I am Ghast. Are you ready for this?' he said in an Eastern European accent.

'Yes, I'm as ready as I'll ever be.' I said.

'Ok, what is going to happen is I bite you here on your neck. I drain off some blood, just a little, this introduces the vampire saliva into your blood. Next, you drink from me. Just a little too, it does not need to be like movies. You're not trying to drain me. This blood will activate the vampire saliva. Your genes, they are altered, you become a vampire and are cured. You are last customer of the night so that is that, then we go into the next room where there is a metal party. Ok?' said Ghast.

Me and Lucas looked at each other and smiled. I looked back at Ghast and smiled.

'Ok,' I said.

So it happened just the way he said. He bit me and, like he said, only drank a little bit of blood. He then made a tiny incision on his wrist and I drank about a mouthful of blood from him.

It burned and I felt all my internal organs tingle. Then he stepped toward the doors and swung them open. The sound that came through that door was amazing. The room must have been soundproofed to fuck.

'Yeah mother fuckers!' said Ghast and, grabbed our wrists and dragged us in.

It was incredible there was a band and people head banging, dancing around, and having fun. There was all this crazy shit going on too. There were people climbing among the roof supports and climbing the walls. I saw Tracy sit on the lap of this woman and bite her neck. There were dancers in cages, other people in S&M gear rolling around on the floor, and people being led around on chains.

After about an hour my body was racked with pain. I stumbled into a corner and collapsed. I must have passed out because when I came back around Val, Tracy, Ghast, all the other party people were gone. I never saw Lucas again either. I assume they took him with them or killed him. I'm hoping it's the former. That was five weeks ago. I couldn't go home, not like this. I've tried to find other vampires but they won't come near me. They just call me a ghoul and weak strain. I've had to fend for myself ever since. I think it might have been something to do with the chemo and the meds. The combination of the things in my body must have fucked up the change," he said.

"What the hell were you thinking, kid? No self-respecting vampires would sell their abilities. They were obviously weak-blooded, multi-digit generation vampires looking to make some quick cash out of you. They just wanted your money," I said.

"I know, if something seems too good to be true, it usually is," he broke down and his breath came in fitful sobs as he continued. "But I was desperate, man. I was gonna die at twenty years old. I didn't want to die...now, I'm this...this thing, this fucking whatever the fuck I am."

I felt sorry for this kid, I really did, but there was no way I would have ever comforted him. Even in his state, he was still a dangerous vampire. Then he looked up at me with his tear soaked face and his eye that was nearly fully regenerated. He spoke words that will stay with me to the day I die.

"Please, please, just kill me. I didn't want to be this. I've been told that when you become a vampire you forfeit your soul. I might not see any kind of afterlife but I don’t care. I'd rather be nothing. Please, have mercy on me. End my misery,” he said.

He bowed his head and I pressed the barrel of my shotgun against the back of his skull. My hands shook and for one of the only moments in my life as a soldier, police officer and dangerous person hunter, I hesitated.

“For what it’s worth, son, I'm sorry,” I said.

“It's ok,” he whispered and lightly nodded his head.

I squeezed the trigger. The shot cracked the silence and tore a little hole in my thick skin. I let a few tears run down my face and stood there with my arms limp at my sides for a moment before I regained my composure. He hadn’t even burned up. He just fell into ash that lay on the floor where he had been along with some lead shot. I got to work and swept them up then put them into a hazardous materials bag. I collected my equipment from the basement, returned it all to my car and went to see Dr Green in the hospital.

“Did you find him?” she said.

“Yes, he’s gone. I had to eliminate him. You were right by the way, he was a vampire, made from a heavily diluted strain. How are your members of staff?” I said.

“They are getting better already,” she said and gestured to Nurse Claire Jones who was sat up in bed and eating soup. “Thank you, Mr V. They should all make a full recovery in the next day or so,” she said.

“You’re welcome. If you ever need our help again, don’t hesitate. You have our number,” I said.

“Thank you, I will,” she said with a smile.

I smiled then made my way back to my vehicle and drove back to base. I reported to George Lawson, filed the report, and deposited the hazardous materials bag in the containment department. I then clocked out and went home.

I showered and scrubbed all the ash, dirt and sweat off my skin. As I watched the dirty water swirl down the drain I thought about Danny. He was hard-done by and life dealt him a losing hand. I hope in death he found the ‘some kind of afterlife’ he was looking for.

I doubt his parents will still be alive after all these years, but Danny may have some surviving family somewhere. If you are that family, you have my sympathies and apologies. I hope this story gave you some kind of closure.

R.I.P. Danny Longridge.

On Video.

A sharp pain in my head brings me around. It throbs from a blow with a dull implement. I open my eyes but all I can see is darkness. I lift my head and a small slither of light reaches my eyes and realise I can see my chest. I now know there is a bag of some sort over my head.

I try to stand up but can barely move my arms and legs. When I do my efforts are met with cold resistance and the clinking sounds of rattling chains. I am shackled to a cold metal chair.

"Hello? Hello? Where am I?!" I shout.

I then hear a voice I don't recognise. It's quiet but not too far away.

"He's awake," the voice says.

"Who's there?!" I say.

Then I hear a voice. This one I do recognise.

"Ok. It's ok. I'll handle this. It's me, Glenn."

Glenn and I had been friends since we were at primary school. He is the only person who knows my secret.

"Glenn! What the fuck is going on?!" I say, trying to keep my voice steady.

"Adam, stay calm. We had to do this. It's for all our sakes," he says.

"Let…let me out! I need to go home," I say.

I'm starting to panic now.

I feel a hand on my head and Glenn pulls the bag away.

"Please, keep calm," he says in a plea as he does it.

"Calm?! How the fuck am I supposed to keep calm? You know what tonight is! I need to get home. I'll be safe there. I need to go. I *need* to go!" I feel the spit fly from my lips as I break into a shout.

"You're safe here," says the other voice.

"Who the fuck is that?!" I say.

A man steps into the light. He has a black ponytail and is dressed in a lab coat, shirt, and jeans. He steps closer until he is stood beside Glenn.

"This is Dr Booth. He runs a website that specialises in documenting people with your, *condition*. He wants to film you for his research. If he can catch you on video he might be able to help you," says Glenn.

"Listen to Mr Hayes. He is a friend. I'm going to record you whilst you have an episode. Then I'll prove to you that all this stuff is in your head. Once you realise that, I can start to help you help yourself," says Dr Booth.

I look from Dr Booth to Glenn and then back again. It's clear that neither of them realises how much danger they are in.

"These chains aren't strong enough to hold me," I say.

“They are hardened stainless steel. Don't worry, Mr Walker. You won't be able to break out of them,” says Dr Booth with a smug smile.

“Why are you not taking this seriously?!” I scream on the brink of hysteria. “These chains are not strong enough! You need to both go now! Run, get in Glenn's van and get the fuck out of here now! Right now! Please!” I scream.

A bolt of pain shoots through the entire length of my body. My jaw clenches shut and my body spasms.

“We are not going anywhere, Mr Walker, and neither are you. You need to calm down and...”

I cut the Dr off mid-sentence as an uncontrollable scream bursts from my open mouth.

“Please, Adam, calm down. It's going to be ok,” says Glenn.

“Your screaming is useless. We're miles outside your town,” says Dr Booth.

I can't hear him as I thrash and writhe against the chains. Another scream bursts from my lungs. I inhale deeply and let out another. It drops in octaves and becomes a roar.

“You are going to see when you watch the video that this is all in your head. All this screaming is nothing more than a manifestation of your mental illness,” says the doctor.

I squeeze my eyes shut and roar as the muscles of

my arms shift under the skin. My finger and toenails thicken and elongate, becoming claws. The bones in my face crunch and begin to move as my face widens. I hear Glenn scream and the doctor swearing as my jaws and nose push out, elongating my face into a snout. Longer, sharper teeth erupt out from my gums and push the others aside. I open my eyes and I see the Dr frozen with fear. The muscles of my limbs bulge and expand as thick fur grows from every follicle.

"Those chains aren't gonna hold!" screams Glenn. The Dr doesn't answer, he just stands there shaking his head.

I throw my arms up and the chains snap like plastic. The wolf is in control now. Adam is just a passenger to its horrifying rage. Reality falls away as everything becomes dream-like and fades into darkness.

I slowly wake with a fierce hangover. I look around and I am lying face down on a forest floor with the sun just rising over the trees. There is that old familiar taste like iron and pork in my mouth. I force myself to stand up and notice I am covered in dried blood. There is something gripped in and twisted around my fingers. I raise my hand and look at it. It's a black ponytail with part of a human scalp still attached to it. I open my hand and shake it free.

I wander around for half an hour to get my bearings and come across an old dilapidated house. Outside there are a few pieces of glass scattered across the ground and a set of deep tyre tracks where someone has driven away at high speed.

I step through the front door and it's clear that someone has died here. The smell of viscera hangs in the air and there is blood on every surface. Inside the first room, I find a torn and bloodied lab coat, two human fingers that have been torn from a hand, and a foot still inside a sock and shoe that hand been gnawed off at the ankle. Other than that there are no other signs of Dr Booth. I look around a bit more. The chair I had been chained to is torn to pieces. I find the camera in the corner of the room. The lens is broken and the viewing screen has been snapped off but the main body of it has survived with just a few scratches. In another room, I find a bag with a t-shirt, a pair of tracksuit pants and a pair of sandals. I put them all on, slip the camera into my pocket and walk out of the front door.

I follow the tyre tracks to find my way out of the forest and make my way back home. The first thing I do, after locking the front door, is switch on my computer and plug the camera into it. While it downloads the files I have a much needed shower. I get out and dry off. I look at the computer screen and see that the download is complete. I can now find out what Dr Booth caught on video.

Reunion.

I've watched the rise of this computer age and tried to embrace it but I am a man of advancing years and so a little slow

er to keep pace with the younger generations. I am intrigued by all this new technology and these smartphones. And so, I have bought myself one. I don't know what all the functions do yet but I am having fun learning.

Anyway, I downloaded a few apps amongst which one of them was this Facebook. I don't know a lot of people on there but I do have a few friends. One of whom was a lady I met in my youth a long time ago. I logged in a few days ago and she had sent me a message. It read:

'Hello, Andrew.
How are you? I am so glad to have found you on here as I have thought of you many times since we separated. I am curious to know where life has taken you. I married a man after you left but I am now a widow of many years.
Hope to hear from you soon.
Geraldine.'

Geraldine and I were introduced by our parents and quickly fell in love. We spent a whole summer courting and enjoying each other's company. Many of our days were spent just walking in the gardens of her family's newly built coastal home near the beach in Crosby. It was a beautiful building hewn from local sandstone and freshly sawn oak. The walls were ornately carved by a local stonemason and it even had its own tower.

Unfortunately, after that summer my work had taken me across the country. We had whispered sweet nothings and promised to keep writing to each other. She even gave me a gift to remember her by. I told her that one day I would come back and marry her. However, like many young lovers in unfortunate situations like ours, life got in the way and eventually we lost contact.

I had tried to find her many times over the years but upon every attempt I had found no trace of her. So I was happy to hear from her and decided to message her back.

'Hello, Geraldine.

I am very well, thank you for asking. I have tried to make contact with you many times over the years, alas, all my efforts ended in vain.

I eventually managed to buy the company that so cruelly took me away from you. After a long time, I took my well-earned retirement and fulfilled my lifelong wish of travelling the world.

I am now living not all that far from my old family estate. Though the old house has gone due to man's perpetual need to innovate. My family's land has been swallowed up by the continuing expansion of the city of Liverpool. I did take a wife but sadly I too have been a widower for many long years.

I never did forget about you. I always kept your love securely concealed within my heart. I hope you do not think it improper of me to reveal this information to you. I also hope it is not inappropriate for me to request that we meet up again.

Andrew.'

She replied a few minutes later:

'Hi, Andrew.

As fate would have it I am living in Liverpool, so probably not too far from you. No, it's not rude of you to tell me that. Truth be told I never forgot about you either. I would love to meet you again. How about at my old family home on Monday at 9.30 pm?'

I was so happy when I read this message. Monday evening soon arrived and I arranged for a taxi to take me to Crosby. Upon arrival, I walked in the cool coastal evening air to the location where I remembered her old family home to be. I was met with nothing more than literal ruins that had been claimed by the sands of the beach. It looked of a similar size but surely this could not be the same building. Then in what used to be the entrance I saw the figure of a woman with a shawl over her head and so I approached her. As I got closer she lowered the shawl and I saw that she was undoubtedly my Geraldine. To my astonishment, she had barely aged a day.

"Hello, Andrew. It's so good to see you," she said.

"I can't believe I'm meeting you again. You look incredible," I said.

She laughed and it sounded just as sweet as it had when we were so young and happy together.

"I was worried that you would speak the same way as you write," she said.

"What can I say, old habits die hard. I try to keep up with current fashions in the way I speak but the writing is deeply ingrained," I said and laughed. "Seriously though, you look amazing."

"As do you. You look just like I remember you. It's all thanks to the gift. You remember the gift I gave you don't you?" she said.

"I do. Thanks to you I have sampled the blood from humans on all continents and in almost every country in the world," I said.

“Wow. You have been having fun,” she said.

“Yep. I just decided that I should see the world for a few years. I went away and now I am back this place has completely changed. It's a shame about your family home. Was there an accident?”

“No. It just fell into ruin. The family fortune dwindled and unfortunately, I had to let it go. It's a historical site now,” she said.

“Historical? I didn't know such young buildings could be classed as historical sites,” I said.

“Andrew, how long have you been away for?” she said.

“Well, I left this town and worked my way up through the company for about twenty years. I then ran the company for forty years until I retired and went travelling. I spent about fifty years or so soaking in all the world has to offer. So, about one hundred and ten years I'd say; give or take,” I said.

“My word. Andrew. You've been gone a lot longer than that,” she said.

“What do you mean?” I said.

“I haven't seen you in over four hundred years!” she said.

“What? Really?” I said.

“Yes, really,” she said.

“I must have been having more fun than I realised. That hike across Russia and China must have taken a lot longer than I thought,” I said with a laugh.

"Come on," she said and took me by the hand. "We have so much to catch up on."

The Boss.

Set into the centre of the heavy wooden door in a stained glass window was the name "McCall's". I pulled it open, walked into the establishment and approached the bar. Stood behind it and drying a glass with a towel stood Sammy Walson.

"Hey, Sammy. Gimme a double on the rocks," I said.

"No," said Sammy.

"What the fuck do you mean 'no'? Give me a fucking drink you little shithead!" I said.

"No. You ain't drinkin' today," he said.

"Who the fuck are you to decide if I'm drinkin' or not? Gimme my drink now you little punk!" I said, about to explode.

"You've got a meeting with the boss," he said with a wry smile.

"Mr Holmes?" I said, a little confused as I had no prior knowledge of any meeting.

"No. The Boss, everyone's boss. You can have coffee, a soft drink, or water," he said.

My heart thumped against my ribs like it was gonna pop right out of my chest and run away like the alien in that movie. This bar, this street, hell, this whole city was owned by Mr Stonebrook. Around here he was 'the big deal', 'the boss man'. He might as well have been God himself. He owned everybody, and he owned their respect too. That's why we called him Everyone's Boss.

"I'll take a cup of that lukewarm, brown piss you call coffee," I said.

"This right here is the best coffee in the city," he said as he poured me a cup.

"If I want good coffee I'll go to your mum's house," I said.

"I always thought you went there to see my dad," he said smiling from ear to ear.

"Cheeky, little mother fucker," I said, unable to stop my frown from breaking into a big, stupid grin. He passed me the cup and I had barely taken one sip when Mr Holmes pulled open the door at the far end of the bar.

"Jackie. I'm glad you got here on time. I see Sammy's keeping you sober as I instructed. Ok, Jackie, don't worry. Your ass isn't on the line here. Mr Stonebrook just wants to talk to you. He does this every so often. Just wants to check up on everyone who is working for him. Just keep a cool head and tell him how well things are going," said Mr Holmes.

"Can I at least finish my coffee?" I said.

"Take it with you. You don't want to keep him waiting," he said.

I walked through the door and down the short corridor. There was a door on one side and across from that one staircase led down to the basement and another up to the 2nd floor. At the end stood the door to Mr Holme's office. I stopped and knocked on it. From the other side came a voice that had once had an Irish accent but was now interwoven with a deep Brooklyn twang.

"Yes, come in," it said.

I opened the door and stepped into the room. Behind the big, and dare I say obnoxious, desk sat an old man who was probably somewhere in his mid-eighties. He was dressed in the most expensive-looking suit I have ever seen. Even though the room was dimly lit he wore a pair of dark Oakley sunglasses. They fit his face so closely they could have been made for him. Lastly, perched between his wrinkled lips was a Marlboro Red which jerked up and down as he spoke.

"Come on in and take a seat, son," he said.

I did as I was told.

"You know who I am?" he said.

"I do, sir," I said.

"Good, that's what I like to hear. If your reputation doesn't proceed you what is the point in having a reputation? I know who you are too," he said.

As he spoke smoke drifted from his mouth.

Sometimes in this business, depending on who is saying it, the last line he said can mean you're about to get arrested, you're about to die, or worse. And believe me, dying is a mercy compared to some of the fucked up shit I've seen happen to people.

"Don't look so shocked," he continued. "I like to know everyone who works for me. It comes with the territory. Jackson Mckellen, thirty-eight years old, five feet ten, originally from Louisville, Kentucky, spent some time travelling from place to place, but now living right here in Brooklyn, New York City. You have been working for my associate, Mr Holmes, for about six months now. How are you finding the work?" he said.

He took the cigarette from his mouth and stubbed it out in an odd shaped bowl. Straight away he took another from the packet, placed it between his lips, and lit it.

"I'm enjoying the work. Your clients are a lot more cooperative than those of other employers I have worked for. So, the work up to now has been a lot less...hands on," I said.

"That's good. I'm glad to hear they have been behaving for you. Would you have any trouble with persuading them to cooperate if you had to?" he said.

"No, sir. I worked for Mr Savini in Los Angeles for three years before his reign ended. There were some clients I had to persuade to pay. A little force was applied and soon they were very compliant," I said.

"Good, good. That's what I like to hear," he said. He took another pull from his cigarette.

"One thing that is different is the form in which you take payment from your clients. I have worked in protection before but have never seen the little black boxes they pay you with. I was just wondering..." I said.

"What's in those little black boxes?" he said in an exhalation of smoke.

"Yes, sir," I said.

"I offer my clients contracts of protection and help for a price. Sometimes that is a monetary payment, and sometimes, well, let's just say some contracts are honoured with less tangible assets. You understand?" he said with an evil smile.

I looked at him for a moment. I've been in the business long enough to understand when people are telling you to stop prying.

"Yes sir," I said.

"What happened to Mr Savini?" he said as he stubbed out his cigarette and lit another.

"His empire got too big for him to control. He made the mistake of not exerting his power enough in the territory he had taken. He got complacent and got too soft on the rivals he had toppled. Too many of them were still alive and they came back to bite him in the ass," I said.

"You wouldn't have had anything to do with his fall, would you?" he said.

"No, sir. Truth is, I liked Mr Savini. He was a nice guy but in the end that was his downfall. It was a real shame what happened to him. His family were receiving the packages of his body parts for weeks," I said.

"Yeah. That's one hell of a way to send a message," he said.

"Quite literally, yeah," I said.

"You, er...you didn't have anything to do with his death did you?" he said with a raise of his eyebrows behind a thin cloud of smoke.

"No, sir," I said.

"Good. That's good. You know, there are vermin all over this city. Before I moved to this country and got into this business I worked as a ratter. I would hunt down rats and catch them. Of course, back in those days, there was no rat poison so we had to kill them ourselves. One time I forgot my knife and my boss wouldn't lend me his so you know what I did?" he said.

"What did you do, sir?" I said.

"I pulled their horrible little heads off with my bare hands," he said with a hint of a smile.

"Christ!" I said.

"No, he certainly wasn't there," he said with a grin. "I still pull rats heads off when I catch them.

It's amazing how much the threat of death loosens their tongues."

He took another pull on his cigarette and looked at me. Even though I couldn't see his eyes through the lenses of his sunglasses I could tell he was looking directly into my eyes. For possibly the first time in my life, I was stunned into silence. His air of authority was tangible. Within the room, an atmosphere of foreboding grew to hellish proportions. I watched as he stubbed out his cigarette into that strange bowl.

"I've seen you eyeing this. Do you know what it is?" he said.

"No sir," I said.

He turned the bowl round to face me and I really do mean face me. The hollow eye sockets, empty nasal cavity and boney grin of the upper teeth of a human skull were all present.

"You know what this is now?" he said.

"Is it ceramic or some sort of resin?" I said.

"Oh no. It's the real deal, alright. My question should really have been. Do you know *who* this is?" he said.

A cold chill ran down my spine.

"I...er...I don't know…sir," I stammered.

He pulled his sunglasses down his nose a little so I could see his eyes. There was no white in those horrendous eyes. Where the white should have been they were dark orange. The Iris' were golden around the outer edge that became neon-yellow towards the centre. In the middle large, cross-shaped pupils looked out at me.

"This is the defleshed skull of the last person who tried to fuck me over. One Mr Paulo Savini. You wouldn't try to fuck me over would you, Jackie?" he said.

"N- n-no, sir. No, I would not," I said.

"Good. That's good. I think we both understand where you stand in this relationship," he said as he held up his left hand. He then tapped the centre of the palm with the index finger of his right hand. He smiled that evil smile and blew smoke from his nostrils and between his teeth. It dawned on me that he didn't have a lit cigarette. Despite this, the smoke had continued to ebb and wisp from his mouth as he spoke to me.

"Ok, Jackson. It's good to have met you, son. I'm happy you are working for me. I just need you to sign this contract," he said as he placed a pile of neat papers in front of me.

What could I do? This man, this thing, had me by the balls. I signed the contract and pushed it back across the desk towards him. He stared at me with those monstrous eyes as his slid his glasses back up to his face.

"Nice doing business with you. That's it, we're

done here. Go on back through to the bar and have a drink on me. You've earned it," he said in such a nonchalant way that I could tell that the past few minutes were just a normal day to him. As for me, I felt numb, what had I just done? I stood up and without a word walked back through to the bar.

"How did it go?" said Mr Holmes.

I looked up at him in what felt to me like a dream. I was in a cold sweat and my skin felt clammy.

"Ah, shit. Go sit down," said Mr Holmes, he looked over at Sammy. "Get Jackie a stiff drink!" he turned back me. "Look, kid, I know this is a lot to take in but you're in the family now. You're safe. No one is ever gonna fuck with you again. You'll never have to worry about bills again. You'll never do time again. You're on easy street now."

"But at what cost?" I said and looked him dead in the eyes.

"Hey come on, Jackie. There weren't any of us going to get into heaven. At least now you know you're on good terms with the boss of the other place. Look, go and sit down, have a drink. You'll see you've made the right decision soon enough," he said.

He slapped me on the back and walked through the door to the back. I skipped the bar, walked straight into the gents and threw my guts up. When I finished I threw up some more. Then I picked my sorry ass up and went to the bar.

"Sammy, give me a double Woods rum, neat," I said.

"Fuckin A!" he said.

He measured it out and I downed it in one. It burnt hot coals and kicked like a mule but it's what I needed.

"Hit me," I said.

"You know the deal then?" he said.

"Oh yeah," I said.

This time he didn't measure it, he just upended the bottle and poured out damn near a full glass.

I'm still working for Mr Stonebrook. What the fuck else am I going to do? It's not like I could just walk away or hand in my notice. He'd be able to find me wherever I went. Who would believe me if I told them who and what he is? And even if they did, what power would they have against him? So, yeah, I'm still working for him. Not much more I can do, and I don't much like the thought of having my head pulled off. I get it, I do. Everyone feels their job is the worst and that their boss is the devil incarnate. Thing is in my case, that's the truth.

Night Security

My name is Wesley Baxter. I work for an agency that hires out night security guards to companies that don't employ any of their own.

One night in August last year I was working at a company named Sandhower Distribution in Bolton. It started out like any other normal night. I arrived at 9 pm, put my jacket, bag, and packed lunch in my locker and made my way to the cabin. I sat watching the monitors for an hour and made a patrol round at 10 pm. I returned to the cabin, made a pot of coffee and sat down to watch the monitors again while I read a book. A few hours passed and I was preparing to make another round when I heard a sound from somewhere within the warehouse. A few moments passed and I heard it again. It was a woman's scream, and it sounded close. I looked out of the window but saw nothing. I looked back at the monitors and manually switched through the cameras.

The night vision cameras from the North sector picked up a figure shambling down one of the aisles between the huge shelves. The strange thing was she wasn't triggering the lights which are all movement-activated. If someone walks through the building at that time at night you can track their movements as the lights switch on and switch off.

I picked up my torch and stepped out of the door. As I walked through the warehouse the light switched on above me. I made my way towards the North sector and noticed the lack of any internally generated sounds. I could hear cars on the road nearby but inside there was nothing besides my own footsteps. There was nothing that would indicate that someone else was in the building with me.

After five minutes of strolling the floor of the building, I reached the North sector. I walked along the aisle where I had seen the woman on the camera and the light switched on. So now I knew they weren't malfunctioning. As I came towards the end of this aisle I heard footsteps further ahead of me. I followed them as they moved down another aisle of shelves but still didn't activate the lights. So, I stopped and stood still and the footsteps continued. I shone my torch to light up the area ahead of me.

About fifty feet away a woman shambled along facing away from me in the middle of the aisle. She was dressed in old tattered clothes and swayed slightly from side to side as she moved.

"Excuse me. Hello. Are you ok?" I called out to her.

She stopped stood in place for a moment before she slowly turned around to face me. I have never seen anything so horrendous in all my life. There was a deep, vertical wound that split her face completely in two from deep in her hairline to the larynx in her neck. Her eyes were wild, her mouth hung open and her bloody tongue hung down between the bisected halves of lower jaw. Her lips pulled back away from her teeth and she let out a horrendous, blood-curdling scream. It was both shrill and hoarse at the same time as if she had been screaming for hours. She then began to stumble towards me. She looked like she had been in an accident and I was about to rush back to the cabin to call for an ambulance. Something about this whole situation didn't seem right though, I mean, how had she gotten inside the building? Why was she not triggering the lights?

I began to back away but as I did she screamed again and charged at me. I turned and ran but I could hear her footfalls gaining on me. It was weird, they were no longer those of a woman. They sounded like a twenty stone man wearing hobnail boots. I was running as fast as I could but it wasn't fast enough. She struck from behind and sent me sprawling into a set of shelves. I lay there dazed for a moment before I caught my senses and could see her striding towards me. Her breath was ragged like she was in a rage. I tried to get up but before I could she grabbed me by my throat and dragged me to my feet. She then lifted me from the floor and held me up with my toes barely skimming the floor. I choked and spluttered as I struggled to breathe. What breath I could get was filled with her stench. Her skin looked like it was rotten and beginning to fall away. Her breath was rancid, like vomit and sulphur, and being huffed into my face. One side of her jaw was clenched shut in a grimace while the other side snapped and gnashed like she was trying to bite me. She screamed one word at me.

"Leave!"

I will hear that voice in my nightmares until the day that I die.

She then threw me away from her like I was weightless. I hit the floor and slid and again she came striding towards me. I scrambled to my feet and ran like hell. The main exit door was twenty feet away from me so I bolted for it. I heard her heavy footfalls gaining on me but I burst through the doors and ran out into the sparsely lit car park. I looked back expecting to see her following me but she just stood at the door with a manic smile on one side of her face and a twisted grimace of anger on the other. As the door slowly shut I saw her dissipate in a swirl, like smoke from a fire, and she was gone.

I ran to my car, took my phone from my pocket and rang my manager at the agency. I heard him pick up but didn't wait for him to speak.

"Alan, you better ring the owner of Sandhower Distribution right now because there is no way in the fucking world that I was going back into that building!" I said.

"Wesley, what the hell are you talking about?" he said.

"Someone broke into the building and attacked me. I didn't get a good look at them but they threw me out and locked the doors," I said.

Of course I lied, I wasn't going to tell him what I saw.

"Ok. I'll…er…I'll call them now and get them to send someone over there," he said.

The company owner turned up with the police in tow. They questioned me and searched the building but besides the damage where I had been thrown into the shelves they found no one inside and nothing was missing. The surveillance footage was corrupted somehow. As soon as the figure begins to stumble into view the video becomes distorted and then cuts out. My injuries and the state of shock I was in when they found me convinced them that I was not involved. I was taken to hospital for observation overnight and allowed to go home the next day.

I still work for the agency but I have never been back to Sandhower Distribution. I was informed that the agency no longer hires out our staff to them either. It's a direct result of something that happened there after my experience.

There was a fatality among the company's day staff. Some poor guy was attacked by something within the building and died. Apparently, he looked like he had been mauled by a fucking bear.

I don't know what the thing was that attacked me, but I know this. It wasn't a woman and I don't think it was a ghost either. I do, however, know I am lucky to be alive.

Many

Every few months I like to take a few days off work and hike into the forest and up the mountains near my home. The last time I went, I saw what looked like the possible head of a new path that I had not explored before. However, on that occasion, I was showing some friends how to get to the lake within the perimeters of the Snowdon National Park. So, I decided that next time out there I would do a bit of exploring. I put in a holiday request at work the day I got back. The months passed as I waited for those precious few days to roll around.

I had packed my clothes, waterproofs, cooking equipment, bedding, and tent into my huge camping backpack a few days before. On the Friday morning, I made some final checks before putting the backpack in my car. I kissed my wife, Kelly, goodbye and set off for a few days of adventure.

Finding the mystery path was the easy part. I had parked my car in the usual spot, changed my shoes, and heaved my pack up onto my back. I set off towards the lake just after 10 am.

The new path spurred off the main path to the left about a mile before the lake. I turned onto it and followed it for about two miles. It seemed just like the other paths in this forest and there didn't seem to be anything unusual about it until it started to narrow and wind its way up the mountain. I'm an experienced hiker and mountaineer, so I continued to follow it and see what I could find.

Soon I could hear the sound of flowing water and

came to a small waterfall. I decided to stop there for a while, took some photos, and ate a light lunch. Soon, I was on my way again. Some thin trees had fallen across the path. Some people say you shouldn't cross natural barriers for superstitious reasons, but I don't believe in such things. So, I climbed over them and continued on my way.

The sun began its downward path toward the horizon, but the density of the trees here prevented me from seeing this, and all too soon it was getting dark.

I found a clearing large enough for my tent and decided to pitch up for the night. I took off my backpack and took out my tent. I removed it from its bag and shook it out, then laid it down on the grass. I then walked around it, pulling it out into a square, ready for the fibreglass poles. I stepped towards the area furthest from the path and my foot slipped through a hole that was covered over by grass. I tried to catch hold of a tree branch or a handful of the grass but before I knew it my entire body slipped down through the hole, and I was tumbling down a steep incline. I landed hard a few times and let out yelps of pain. I played rugby in my youth and was familiar with the feeling of bones breaking. It still bloody hurts though. Some of my fingernails were ripped free in my efforts to slow or stop my descent. I was getting dizzy and felt sick, then felt a heavy blow to the back of my head. The world became blurry, and I blacked out. I have no idea how much time passed. Though, I think it was no more than a few hours. I came back to near consciousness a few times. One time it was dark, another time it was light. I had dreams of bugs and things biting me and wiggling all over me. Eating me, slivering, and scratching around inside my skull. Finally, I felt rain against my face. I tried to open my eyes. The lids fluttered for a few seconds and then opened. I looked up into the canopy of the trees. I was lying on my back at the bottom of a deep ravine. My head lay at an awkward angle against a rock. I moved to sit up and winced at a surge of pain in my neck. I rocked my head from side to side and felt the bones click and scrape against each other. Slowly it then began to feel better. I pushed myself up with my hands, then got my feet underneath me. My knees felt loose and weak at first, but then they tightened up, and I was able to get to my feet. I stumbled around for a few steps but my balance began to return. I told myself I should take it easy. If I had a head injury I could have a concussion, among other things. I put my hand in my pocket and took out my phone. I pressed the on button, but nothing happened. I held the button down, but still nothing. Somehow the battery was completely dead. It had been fully charged when I set out earlier. I had 1 checked the time when I stopped to make camp and I had at least 70% charge then. I put my phone back in my pocket, and the weight of it caused it to tear through the material. I looked down at my clothes and saw they were dry but were threadbare and starting to rot in places.

"What the fuck? How long have I been out here?"

I said aloud to myself.
My voice sounded dry and raspy. I had water in my backpack. I looked up the wall of the ravine. There was no way I would be able to climb back up there without equipment. So I started to walk along the bottom of this ravine with the intention of finding my way back to the place where I had decided to set up camp. My plan was to collect my belongings and head home. It took me five hours to push through the thick, seldom traversed, foliage of the forest just to find the start of the path again. It would take another six hours of walking to get to my belongings. My house was only two hours walk away in the opposite direction. The decision was an easy one.

An hour later I was standing in the car park, but my car was nowhere to be seen. I walked back and forth a few times and looked at all the cars that were parked but I was right, my car was gone. Anger grew inside me. Some arsehole had stolen my car. I couldn't believe it. It was a shitty old hatchback. I have no idea why the hell would anyone would want to steal it. I looked up to the sky.

"Hello. Can you make this day a bit fucking worse, please? No phone, now this shit too? Fuck sake!" I said aloud.
This anger wasn't getting me anywhere. Home was a four mile walk away, but it was already getting dark. I had no choice but to keep going.

The night was colder than it had been the night before and although I saw a few people from afar there weren't many people on the street.

"It's not Halloween yet," a group of teenagers called to me from the other side of the road. I smiled and stuck up my middle finger to which they all laughed. I must have looked like a real mess though. Muddy and scratched up with torn clothes. I'm not surprised they thought it was a costume.

By the time I reached my front door it was dark. I took my keys from my pocket and unlocked the door. The house was in darkness too but I could see well enough. I walked up the stairs and went into the bathroom. I switched on the light and looked in the mirror. My face looked strange. My cheeks were gaunt and I was covered in dirt and blood. My eyes looked odd. I turned on the tap and let the basin fill with water. I then washed the blood and dirt from my skin. It felt dry and leathery. Not like I remembered. The back of my head throbbed so I reached my hand up and touched the area. There was definitely a wound back there but how bad it was I couldn't tell. I couldn't see it in the mirror from this angle, but It was dry though and was no longer bleeding. A strange thing happened then, I began to remember what happened to me. The fall, the impact to the back of my head. The darkness and the insects. The flies and their eggs. The eating. Many beings becoming one.

Light suddenly seeped under the bottom edge of the bedroom door and I could hear Kelly moving around inside. The door opened so I stepped onto the landing to greet her. With the light coming from behind me she must have only been able to see my silhouette. Because she came out of the bedroom

with a baseball bat held over her head.
…"Whoever you are, get the fuck out of my house!" she yelled.
…"Woah! Kelly, it's me, Mark," I said.
Upon hearing my voice she froze and lowered the bat.

"M-Mark. Where the hell have you been?" she said.

"I've only been out since yesterday morning," I said.

"It's been four months," she said.
She dropped the bat and stepped towards me.

"We all thought you were dead?" she said as she switched on the light.
She stopped and screamed. Maybe it was my gaunt face, or my mottled skin stretched across my skull and bones. Or maybe it was the far too many insect eyes looking out from the sockets that used to only contain two human eyes.

"What are you?! What happened to you?!" she said.

"I fell down a ravine. My body was broken and my skull cracked open. I should have died but I was saved. The bugs and insects ate my flesh, my brain, my mind. They absorbed me. We became one. I'm still me, I'm still Mark. Just different is all," I said.
I smiled and felt the maggots wiggling in my gums. Kelly raised the bat in preparation to swing it at my head. I flew out from the back of my head as hundreds of flies swarmed around her to stop her, to make her see that I am all these bodies, that I am still alive. She waved her arms and stumbled back.

Her foot waved in the open air beyond the top step. I landed on her with all my bodies and flapped my wings to pull her back to safety, but it was not enough. She fell and landed awkwardly as she tumbled down the stairs. Bones snapped, muscles tore and joints twisted into unnatural angles. It took seconds but the damage was done. I pulled all my bodies back to my human one and ran down the stairs.

"No, no, no! Kelly, shit," I cried out.

I crouched down next to her. She lay there crumpled and still. Her head twisted and flexed too far. I began to cry, but as I lay my hand on her side, I noticed she was still breathing. I realised at that moment that I could save her just like the insects saved me. I crawled all my little bodies onto her and began to eat.

It’s just business.

I always loved southern Spain at this time of year. Early July, just before it started to get too hot for my liking. August was a no-go for me. The heat would be stifling by then with no reprieve from the heat even in the shade.

The annual conference for Integrated Computer Technologies International was being held here, and I was determined to talk one to one with Peter Weller, the head of the UK sector of the company.

I exited my room and walked down through the hotel to the pool area. I spotted him there on a sun lounger by himself with a spare lounger next to him. I eagerly walked to the spare lounger intent on getting there before anyone else.

“Hello, Mr. Weller. Is this lounger taken?” I said.

Peter peered at me through half-open eyes behind his designer sunglasses.

“No. All yours if you want it,” he said.

On a table between us, beside the several empty glasses from the cocktails he had drunk this morning, stood his bottle of sun lotion.

I placed my bottle of sun lotion on the table beside his and sat down on the lounger. I made myself comfortable and took the sun lotion from the table. I applied some to my body and placed the bottle on the floor on the other side of my lounger.

“Fantastic location for a conference, isn't it,” I said.

Peter looked over at me for a second.

“Yes, most wonderful. I assume you're with the

company?" he said.

"Yes. I work in the Surrey branch. Jack Hall. I'm head of accounts and marketing," I said and offered out my hand.

"Peter Weller, head of the UK sector. Well, you already seem to know that," he said with a smug grin as he shook my hand.

"The Ghaldoons have outdone themselves this year. I've been hoping to make some strong business connections and to top up my tan when the opportunity arose, and now I am able to kill two birds with one stone," he said.

The Ghaldoons family owns the entire company.

"Wonderful, isn't it? Thankfully, it's not too hot right now," I said.

He smiled at me almost sympathetically.

"I don't mind the heat. You know what they say. If you can't take the heat, get out of the kitchen," he said.

We both laughed a little.

"Yep, the Hollandier company got themselves out of the kitchen," I said.

"They certainly did," he said.

"It's a shame. All those people's jobs just up in smoke like that," I said.

"On an individual level, it's terrible. Fortunately, I am able to separate myself from that level of connection. It sounds harsh, but it's just business. It's nothing personal," he said.

"Yes, I suppose you're right. It's just the way things go sometimes," I said.

"If it makes you feel any better, we took on a

number of the workers after the collapse. I suppose we should thank Jarad Hollandier in a way. He saved us a lot of money training all those staff members," he said.

"You don't feel any sympathy for Jarad then?" I said.

"No. The man's a fool. He came into this cutthroat business and expected to be able to play the game. He couldn't handle it, and he took a fall," he said.

I nodded in agreement.

"Why did the company fail so badly?" I said.

"Jarad comes from a working class background. He was a no one, a nothing. Then, some distant relative died, and he inherited a sizeable amount of money. Instead of squandering it on big TVs and cars, like most of that sort of people, he invested and started the Hollandier company. They were doing well. Some suggested they were ICTI's biggest rival, which is absurd. Anyway, he came to ICTI to suggest a possible partial merger in exchange for insider information. I took the opportunity to give him some bad information, and the fool ate it up. The next thing his company collapsed," he said the last sentence with a chuckle.

"Do you not feel bad about that?" I said.

"No. I merely put things in place. He used those things to his own demise. Put him back down in the slums where he belongs. Good riddance if you ask me," he said.

He sat up, took the sun lotion, and applied it liberally all over his body. I had to turn my head to keep the smile from my face. He lay back down and smiled at the sun.

"I met him once, you know," I said.

"Who, Hollandier?" he said.

"Yes. Did a little business with him," I said.

"What on earth for? Nothing to do with our company, I hope," he said.

"No. Something unconnected. A bit of a side hustle of mine, if you will. You see, he invested money in other places, too. Weapons development of all things," I said.

"Really? Interesting line of business. A lot of field for manoeuvrability," he said.

"He was telling me about a new weaponised neurotoxin with a high-speed delivery system. They can put it in anything. Liquids, creams, lotions. The sort of things that people use all the time. Let's use sun lotion as an example. The lotion carries it into the outer layers of the epidermis, and the delivery system then allows it to soak deeper into the tissue, then the bloodstream. It doesn't take all that long either," I said.

"I-I can't move," he said.

"First, it causes paralysis. Then the vital organs begin to shut down," I said.

"You, you bastard. Am I going to die? Are you killing me?" he said.

"Not me. Mr. Hollandier is killing you. I'm just a businessman," I said.

"You did this to me," he said.

"Wrong again. I merely put things in place. You decided to use them," I said.

"Do you have an antidote? Whatever he's paying

you, I'll double it, treble it," he said.

"If I took your offer, it would undermine my client's trust, and that would be no good for my business, would it? You're a businessman. You understand that this is nothing personal," I said.

"Wha-what did you sa-say your name?" he slurred in a whisper.

"It's not Jack Hall, and it won't be the name I am booked into the hotel under. It's not even the name printed on my passport. At this point, for you, it doesn't make any difference. Just allow yourself to fall into a nice slumber. By the time anyone realises what has happened, I'll be long gone, and so will you," I said.

"Fug yuh," he slurred just before his eyes closed.

"Good night, Mr. Weller," I said.

I took the poisoned sun lotion from the table and placed it back in my bag. I used my towel to pick up the real bottle of lotion I had placed at the side of my lounger, wiped my fingerprints away, and placed it back on the table. I then stood up and walked away from the pool area and back to my room. I removed my wig and stepped into the shower. The prosthetic nose, cheekbones, and chin I was wearing melted away in the hot water. A few minutes later they were no more than slime running down the plug hole. I stepped out of the shower and dried myself off. I dressed in a shirt and trousers, then left the room and made my way to the reception to check out.

"I hope you enjoyed your stay, Mr. Leon," said the receptionist.

"It was most wonderful, thank you. Very relaxing," I said.

I flashed a smile, walked out to the car waiting at the front of the hotel and was driven to the airport. By the time anyone noticed that Mr. Weller had not just fallen asleep, I was no longer in the country.

Old Photos

I am sitting here sorting my old possessions into storage boxes labelled 'KEEP' and 'THROW OUT' and have come across an old shoebox that I have not seen in many years.

I open it and inside find a treasure trove of old photographs. There are photos of my family at the beach, the zoo, and on holidays in many different countries.

While sifting through them I find one of a child I had not seen for many years. It is me aged seven or eight. As I look at his eyes I remember the joy and wonder the world held for me back then. I didn't understand that a life of work and pain, both physical and emotional, lay before me.

I find myself longing to be that naive and innocent again but alas, that child is gone and the world keeps on turning.

My body has changed a lot since those days of youth. I grew into a man, sporty and athletic. Then old age crept up on me and arthritis and two strokes took their toll on my body.

I look again at the image of young me. I then look at my hands. I flex my fingers and feel the micromotors stir within. When I could no longer walk and talk I decided to have my consciousness transferred to an entire body prosthesis.

I look at that photo and it dawns on me, that body no longer exists. But it is still a photo of me...isn't it?

The Forest.

I lay on the forest floor on the crest of a small hill between two trees. I saw the thing approaching, moving the way I had been told they do. Slowly choosing its path among the undergrowth and trees. Quiet, cold, and calculated. Its eyes moved in its head and it looked directly at me, fortunately, my camouflage and the darkness concealed my whereabouts.

It slowly moved, turning its head from side to side as it raised its foot and placed it back down on the ground without making a single sound. Then it stood motionless like it was listening. My heart sped into a gallop and a cold dread washed over my flesh as I realised it was listening for me. I held my nerve and stood stone still.

I'm not the biggest or the strongest among my family and friends but I am larger than this thing. It's their attack you have to be wary of though. It comes fast, almost without warning, and they almost always move in packs.

It resumed its slow quiet path through the trees and moved past me. When I knew I was out of its eye line I quietly rose to my feet and backed away. I then turned and paced away before launching into a gallop. I turned my head slightly and saw it raise its gun but I was already disappearing into the forest.

About Paul J. Kearns.

Paul J. Kearns is an author from Bolton, Northwest England. He lives there with his wife and two children.

From a young age Paul has had an interest in writing. He is also a fan of all things dark and horrifying.

After leaving school he started working as a dental technician and earned a B-Tec National diploma and a UCHE in Dental Technology from the Manchester Metropolitan University. He still works as a Dental Technician today.

In his spare time he loves to spend time with his family and friends, writing, watching movies, gaming, and drawing.

Dear reader,

I hope you enjoyed reading this book. I hope you enjoyed the stories, and love them or hate them I hope you were drawn in by the characters too.

The oldest story in this book is 'Confined', first being written somewhere around 2012. It was not ready at the time of publishing my previous collection, 'The Hunted and other twisted tales' as I was not happy with it back then. It needed more work so I held it back.

The newest story is 'It's just business' being written

in late 2023. It was written as part of a contest for the Facebook group ‘The Amateur Writers Community’ which is run by my friend, Steven Scholl. As were a few of the other stories in this book.

If you were inspired in any way to write that story you have always been thinking of and keep meaning to write, I would encourage you to go ahead with it. Please don’t wait until you retire, as tomorrow is not promised. Just ten minutes writing every day is a good start. And don’t expect it to be perfect straight away. Good writing takes practice, and work, and rewriting, and reworking, and rewriting, and reworking.

Please tell your friends and family about this book. Word of mouth is an invaluable way for authors to reach a larger audience.

Thank you and happy reading.

And remember, don’t afraid of the dark, be afraid of the things that use it as camouflage.

Printed in Dunstable, United Kingdom

71596580R00102